ONE SUMMER ON MACKINAC

ALANA ROBIN

ARB
press

One Summer on Mackinac

Published by ARB Press LLC

byalanarobin.com

@byalanarobin

Copyright © 2024 by Alana Robin Baumel

First Edition: May 2024

Cover and Internal Design by Alana Robin

Line Edited by Sabrina Grimaldi

ISBN (Print Paperback): 979-8-9904353-1-5

ISBN (eBook): 979-8-9904353-0-8

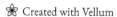 Created with Vellum

To my husband, Chewy –
For showing me that teenage love stories can be everlasting.

places both real and fiction from the novel

ONE SUMMER ON MACKINAC

illustrated by alana robin

ONE

**Mackinac Island Travel Tip #1:
It's pronounced Mack-in-aw, not Mack-in-ack.**

AS THE RADIO began to crinkle with static and the trees lining U.S. Route 23 North flew by the window, I knew we were getting closer. This was going to be it—my first summer alone, living on an island.

Not just any island: Mackinac Island, where horses and bikes compete for the right of way on Main Street and there are more fudge shops than actual restaurants. Situated in the Great Lakes between the lower and upper peninsula of Michigan, this was a place, frozen in time, that provided the perfect escape before entering the real world.

My mom was rattling on from the driver's seat. She was going back and forth between saying she couldn't believe her little Ariella was all grown up and how it was a massive betrayal that I was leaving her three months earlier than originally planned.

"You know you can still change your mind? You don't need to get ahead on—"

I cut my mom off before she could offer to turn this car around for the twelfth time in our four-hour journey.

"I'm sorry, Mom. You know I have to do this. Other people have been working in hospitality their whole lives. They grew up around this. They are practically Eloise. I need to catch up and get actual experience this summer."

I tugged the hot black seat belt away from my neck in an attempt to regain a comfortable position as my mind ran through all the reasons this summer would help me in the fall. In just three short months at the end of August, I would be moving east to begin a hospitality management program at Cornell University. The school had the top program in the world to study hotels, restaurants, and general business management practices. Graduates went on to work for major hotel chains, global airlines, Michelin-starred restaurants, and even in financial services and real estate for all the above.

"I know, but promise me you'll at least try to have a little fun this summer," my mom pleaded. "You have the next four years to be serious and focus on school."

My mom was trying to encourage me to relax, which naturally made me do the opposite, causing my jaw to clench and my back to tense against the faux leather seat.

"Fine, I will," I said, thinking back to the endless websites I'd read about all the things to do on Mackinac Island.

When I searched for the best place to get hospitality training in the Midwest, all signs (and webpages) pointed to the island, featuring all the unique experiences and high-end services offered.

As a person, I was always prepared, and the idea of starting college without a proper job in the industry scared me. It scared me, but not in a *jump-out-from-behind-a-wall-boo* way, but rather in an *anxiety-inducing-up-all-night* way. While I didn't know much about my future classmates, my social media stalking revealed two things. Few would be from the

Midwest, and even fewer would have grown up with zero exposure to high-end hospitality. Their families either owned luxury hotels, or they grew up regularly staying in them.

This summer was my chance to experience it all. Sure, I would be working in a fudge shop on Main Street most days, but I had also been promised the opportunity of shadowing all of the roles in the hotel and learning about hotel operations in my free time. The hours spent at the hotel would even count toward my college credit (a requirement of the School of Hotel Administration for us to receive practical education in addition to our classroom learning) if they were substantial enough. Besides, even if the job didn't turn out to be everything I hoped it would be, I would still be living on an island and saving up money for the fall.

My mom signaled right and started to merge off the highway. In the distance, Lake Huron was creeping into view. There was only a ferry ride left before the summer of my daydreams.

———

PULLING up to the ferry dock, our car was engulfed in a cloud of dust as we wove through the shouting crowds and followed the signage toward the unloading zone. The gravel lot was the epitome of organized chaos with people juggling bags, bikes, and kids as they unloaded and coordinated who would park and who would go buy tickets—all before the next ferry's departure. We were fifth in line and cutting it close on time.

As someone who fully embraced the planning stage of any trip, I was a notorious over-packer. Even after trying to pack lightly, I ended up with two duffle bags, a bike, and a bunch of snacks my mom had insisted I bring in case there wasn't food on the island. I hopped out of the car, gently placing each bag onto the leaning tower of nylon luggage in the neighboring parking space labeled 'Next Ferry.' It was going to be tough to maneuver everything when we got to the island.

"Which hotel are you staying at?" a girl a few years older than me asked as she approached the car with tags and a pen, proudly smiling as if she were the official island welcoming committee.

"I'm not. I am going to be working at Rosanna's Fudge Shop on Main Street," I timidly said as I pulled my purple bike off the back of the car.

"No way! That will be great. I will just tag your bags for Donnie's and someone will meet you on the other side."

I had no idea what Donnie's was, but she hastily scribbled away with a level of confidence that could not be challenged. Especially by me.

"You're going to want to get a license plate for this as soon as you arrive," the girl advised as she tapped the bike with a heavily chewed pen cap and breezed away without another glance back.

"Honey, you need to get in line," my mom said, snapping me back into motion. "If we don't go now, your bags might make it to the island before we do. I'll go park the car and meet you."

She pulled away, searching for a spot that'd fit her champagne-colored mini-van. That mini-van had seen us through countless drop-offs at summer camp and visits to my grandparents' house in New York. It had traveled triple the mileage of most cars its age and had just embarked on the ultimate journey to a summer in northern Michigan. Its next voyage would take me to college. I only hoped the gravel lot would go easy on its old wheels.

Suddenly, I was alone. Before the feeling could sink in, I was swarmed by the throng of tourists wearing fanny packs, carrying helmets, and balancing their bikes and babies. As with everywhere in the Midwest, there was a real mix of attire.

Some people were dressed up in colorfully printed Lilly Pulitzer dresses and others had college t-shirts and ripped shorts with splattered paint stains.

With my own attire blending into the coastline of tourists eagerly awaiting their chariot to the island, I wondered if I would fit in there. I had always had plenty of friends, but having lived in the same split-level house in Ann Arbor my whole life, I seldom approached a situation where I didn't know anyone else. I hadn't made new friends in years. Did I even remember how to?

A loud horn went off three times, causing a communal jump that may have looked like a planned dance, or even the wave, to anyone watching from afar. The sound was the same as a fog horn or a tornado warning, but the sun was shining brightly, reflecting up from the lake. I quickly spun around as the double-decker ferry pulled into the pier.

"ALL ASHORE! NEXT STOP MACK-IN-AW ISLAND," he drew out the ending, signaling the counter-intuitive pronunciation of the French name.

The crowd buzzed with excitement as the waves crashed against the pier and the passengers leaving the island disembarked across the shaky metal platform. The corners of my mouth involuntarily moved upwards as I took in their beaming smiles. The happy vacation memories tucked into their minds were infectious. I could almost see each of their camera reels—dinners overlooking the water, horse carriages up the hilly streets of the island, and bike rides along the water's edge.

"I made it!" my mom joined me in line just as it was our turn to board.

We carefully took the slick metal steps up to the top deck. The ferry jumped from wave to wave, water splashing against the side of the boat, for about 15 minutes. As it turned around the corner of a mass of rocks, the island peeked its way into view. First, a large white hotel atop a hill. Then, an entire main street of pastel-colored buildings, rainbows of bikes, and yellow carriages—drawn slowly forward by horses. The horn blared again as the dock appeared, a mixture of shouts filling the air as the workers guided the ferry closer to it.

Perched on the sidelines of the action, as I all too often was, the whole scene felt like something out of a movie. It reminded me of a movie set in the early 1900s, but a movie nonetheless—a movie where people fell in love for the first time and made everlasting friendships with people from around the world, filled with deep belly laughs and reckless adventures.

It reminded me of a movie where maybe if I got out of my own way for long enough, I could be the next main character...

TWO

Mackinac Island Travel Tip #2:
Find a dock porter to help with your luggage.

AS MY MOM and I stepped off the boat, we were greeted by a row of men on bicycles with metal shelves hanging off the front. They frantically grabbed luggage as soon as the baggage carts were unloaded from the ferry, without any direction or direct communication with the bag owners. I watched in awe as they stacked the bags three high on their handlebars before weaving through the tourists and out onto the main street, somehow knowing where to take things.

"Hey, are these yours?"

Before we could even walk over to my bags, they were swooped up and onto a bike's handlebars by a tall guy with dark, shaggy hair whose half-smirk made me wonder if all my belongings had been replaced with feathers during the ferry ride over. He wore a navy blue polo with a Hotel Waldenwood logo embroidered and khaki shorts. I couldn't help but notice his corded forearms and the stretch of his polo around his unnaturally broad shoulders, a sign that he probably spent his days biking and towing luggage around this motorless island. I guess we wouldn't have to fumble with all my luggage after all...

"Yeah. I'm Ariella. I'll be working at Rosanna's this summer," I smoothed out my t-shirt and athletic shorts, hoping it wasn't too obvious that I had just spent the last four hours in a car.

He looked quite a bit older than me, maybe in his mid-twenties, but I choked back my woes and mustered up my best smile. Maybe he could be my first friend here.

"Sweet. I'm Jared. Follow me," he kicked off the slotted wood dock and out into the chaos of Main Street.

The street was nestled between Inns and shops and teeming with obstacles. Horses. People. Bikes in motion. Bikes discarded at the side of the road. My head was on a swivel trying to take it all in while keeping up with Jared and my mother. I pushed my bike, staying on foot to better dodge the many obstacles of Main Street until we veered down an alley and back toward the waterfront.

"This is it. You're staying in the big apartment with some of the others. I think one other girl will be at the Fudge Shop with you, some of the others work at Donnie's and the hotels. I lived here a few summers ago... It's a great setup."

Jared swung the door open to the three-story weathered, white wooden building and climbed the stairs two at a time with my luggage in tow.

"Sounds great," I said quietly, intimidated by his age, looks, and speed.

Was I seriously going to be living this close to the water?

The stairwell to the apartment was as weathered as the exterior, with light yellow paint peeling from the walls, but otherwise, the apartment was solid. It was dated in a charming way with a large living room filled with mismatched couches and chairs. Each had a different nautical or floral pattern to the upholstery, almost as if they were leftovers from somewhere else.

"Oh wow, Ella, look at this. You have a view of the water."

My mom pushed past me and into the apartment and peered through the large bay window in the living room.

"I am just so jealous. I wish I could stay here for the summer with you. Do you think they have an extra room? I'm just kidding, I know moms aren't allowed. Wow. This will be great though. Oh, look, your roommate has already moved in," my mom buzzed on, exploring the apartment further while Jared and I exchanged brisk goodbyes in the stairwell.

"Well, I'll be seeing you around," Jared winked before disappearing back down the stairwell just as quickly as we arrived.

I kicked myself for not making a more memorable first impression, vowing to leave shy Ella at the door for the rest of the summer. I had always been an introverted extrovert. Shy until I got to know someone and then unable to shut up.

I had often blamed this particular personality trait on my looks. Between my brown eyes, wavy brown hair, and over-sized nose, I was average at best. When I went through puberty a bit before everyone else, rounding out my curvy figure, I had a small boost of confidence from all the attention, but it waned as soon as the other girls escaped their own adolescence.

This summer, I wanted to jump right into extroversion and not hide behind my insecurities. I wanted to push myself out of that comfort zone. I needed to prove to myself that I could do it now, before college. How hard could it really be?

———

AFTER UNPACKING my bags into the dresser, an aged wooden structure that teased to fall apart with each passing movement, and making my bed in my hot pink floral quilt from middle school, I flopped onto the twin bed. My mom was still busy wandering the rest of the four-bedroom apartment and taking inventory of what we would need to pick up at the store.

"Hi, I'm Naomi—Ella's mom. It's so nice to meet you."

The door to the apartment slammed shut as my mom greeted someone in the living room.

"Hey, welcome! Tory. I moved in last month to help with pre-season over at the Inn. I'll be sharing a room with Ella," a tall girl with two pink streaks in her otherwise jet-black hair shook my mom's hand with purpose.

She wore a pencil skirt and a cardigan that conflicted with the shiny diamond sparkling on her nose. I sprang out of the bed disguising my nerves with a soft smile, attempting to make good on my internal promises as I met my new roommate.

After a quick hello, I learned that Tory was 22. She had just graduated from college and would be working the front desk for the summer at the Inn. Her boyfriend still lived down near Detroit and would be visiting throughout the summer, and she hoped I would be comfortable with him sharing our room. My first instinct was to say no, her boyfriend couldn't share this tiny room with us, but—always a perpetual people pleaser—I forced a smile. The brevity in her voice and the confidence that exuded from each sentence she shared told me everything I needed to know about her. Primarily that we have nothing in common.

"No problem. He can totally stay with us anytime."

She also gave me a tour of the apartment and even explained why there was a large piece of duct tape in the shower. It was not there to make sure nothing leaked but was covering a hole that peeped into the shower from one of the other bedrooms. Apparently last summer, the boys that lived in the room got a little drunk and drilled a hole into the shower one night...

Luckily, my mom spent the last 25 years of her life living in a Big Ten college town and was completely unfazed by this development, laughing through the story as if it was merely a victimless prank. Me on the other hand... I was going to be double-checking that tape every day for the next three months.

———

I LOVE MY MOM. We are best friends, and I genuinely mean that. She was going to be heading home tomorrow, so I knew we needed to make the most of our evening together before she left the island and went back to Mackinaw City for the night. Oddly, the name of the city and the island are pronounced the same (MACK-IN-AW) despite having different spellings.

With no real agenda for the evening, Mom and I headed down to the only grocery store on the island. Located at the end of Main Street, the sign claimed it to be the oldest grocery store in America. The inside was quaint with wooden shelves, more similar to a bookstore than a grocery store, and only one to two options per item. The prices were at least three times higher than Kroger's back home.

"Well, I am glad we came prepared with snacks and all your toiletries. It seems like you want to avoid doing any of your big shopping here if you can," my mom lamented, pulling a few items off the shelf that she deemed necessities, even at these prices.

I wandered the aisles, making mental notes of things I might want throughout the summer. I had always loved going to the grocery store. Roaming the aisles. Seeing the choices. The possibility of having anything you wanted, or wanted to eat at least, at the tips of your fingers. I was consistently the first of my siblings to offer to go with my mom growing up.

This store was different though; after wandering three aisles, I had seen all the options it had to offer and was ready to leave the charming shelves behind.

"Mom, should we go to dinner? I know you don't want to end up on the last ferry tonight, and I need to finish getting settled."

"Of course. Let me just get you these parting gifts and then we can pick a spot," she graciously treated me to this last haul of goodies before we ambled Main Street in search of a casual dinner spot.

We weren't exactly sure where we wanted to eat, and my mom had only been to Mackinac Island once before, so it was hard to know what would be the best option. There was mostly a mix of touristy gift shops—the type with t-shirts hanging on the walls—and old-timey inns. Everything on Mackinac was a relic of the past.

Main Street was dotted with people, all peering into restaurants and scrutinizing the menus posted in the windows as they mulled over the direction to take their evenings. I didn't know it at the time, but these crowds were nothing compared to what I would witness later in the summer. We walked down one side of the street and looped back up the other before settling on the Seahorse Bar and Grill. If the restaurant were in any other town, we wouldn't have looked at it twice. But it wasn't just a dive you would pass over in any other town after seeing the beat-up booths and simple menu. It was here, located directly on the water with a sweeping view of the waning sun.

We ordered a whitefish dip to start and burgers for our main course. Every other time I had tried whitefish spread, it was on the East Coast when we were visiting with family for the holidays, but I had never had whitefish dip comparable to this. This dip was fresher with a lemony, scallion flavor and a lot less salt. It was also served hot, which sounded weird but is absolute perfection in a bite. I made a mental note to come back for it later this summer. Maybe with Tory.

After a tearful (my mom, not me) goodbye, my mom caught a ferry back to the mainland for the night. Mackinaw City, the town with the ferry dock where we had parked our car, was directly across the lake, and staying there would make it easier for her to drive home tomorrow morning.

I strolled down Main Street, eyes sparkling in the moonlight, as I took in my new home at night for the very first time. My pulse quickened, new energy filling my body while I imagined what was to come. The lights twinkled from the windows of the hotels and the fudge shops were filled with after-dinner crowds, but the street was clear of bikers for the first time all day. I was grateful for the semi-private moment to savor every small detail. The air filled with sticky sweet chocolate smells. The live music spilled out of the bars. The families laughed as they skipped down the sidewalks hand-in-hand. What kind of memories would I make here this summer? The sugarcoated air supplied me with a sneaking suspicion that they would be good.

As the crowds thinned out, I inferred that, like my mom, all the day trippers had headed back to their hotels across the lake for the evening. It was cheaper to stay over there, and the mainland had a lot of chain options whereas the hotels on the island were a mix of independently owned smaller inns or luxury hotels.

Already unpacked, but with nowhere else to go I managed to find my way back to the big apartment. When I got to the chipped door and pulled out my key, I discovered it was unlocked. The sounds of music and laughter seeped out into the hallway. I had only met Tory earlier, but this was evidently my moment to meet my other roommates. Based on the quick tour, I was guessing there would be three or four others.

I took a deep breath and walked through the door, "Hi, I'm Ella."

"Hey! I'm Andre. This is my brother Chase."

Two boys who looked like they were in their early to mid-twenties stood up from the sinking couch.

"Welcome to the big apartment. We live here, along with Tory and two others who haven't moved in yet. Since we are the only place right on Main Street, everyone likes to come to hang out here. This is Sophie, Mike, and Tory, who you've probably met already."

"You're working in the fudge shop?" Chase, the taller of the two with a friendlier smile, tilted his head to the side as he joined me in the entryway.

I guess I hadn't made many strides to join the group in the living room yet.

"Yeah, I start tomorrow. What about you?"

"Andre and I are at Donnie's—if you crave fries, we've got them. Sophie's at the clothing boutique and Mike is at the Inn with Tory."

"Awesome," I bit my lip, pretending to know exactly which clothing boutique and Inn he was referring to.

There were at least a handful of each right below us on Main Street, but I let it go, assuming I would figure it all out in due time.

"Do you want a beer?" Mike called from the fridge.

Everyone in the room was older than me, probably all 21, and I wondered if he thought I was too or if he just didn't care either way.

I had tried beer before and it wasn't for me.

"I'd love one, but I actually wanted to finish unpacking

before my first day tomorrow. I start at nine, so there's a bunch to do still!"

"No worries. You'll get used to running on five to six hours of sleep," Mike snorted before slamming the rickety fridge shut and returning to the couch with the others.

I fought the urge to check if the fridge door was still on its hinges. The whole kitchen was decrepit as if it hadn't been upgraded in at least 40 years, and the wooden fridge was clearly the only appliance in regular use. The charm of the living room and view made up for it, having distracted me from even noticing the kitchen earlier in the day, but I hoped I wouldn't need to cook often these next few months.

"Great to meet you all," I backed into my room and over to the bed.

Had I made a mistake declining the beer? Would they think I was lame and realize how much younger I was? Would they invite me to have a drink with them again this summer?

As my mind swirled with questions of whether I had just ruined my own summer by being a downer on night one, Tory came in and offered to keep me company while I finished unpacking. The only thing was, I had finished unpacking. This was just an excuse to be alone and avoid saying the wrong thing.

"So, is this your first time working on the island?" I busied my hands unfolding and refolding the clothes in my drawer

"Nope, I was up at Stonebridge last summer. It's up in the woods past the Grand and near the back nine of the golf course. Very cool place, with great tips from all the weddings they host, but the employee housing is up there, and I didn't want to be trapped away from town again this summer. I just graduated, so this is my last fun summer before I go find something to do year-round."

"That's awesome."

"What's your deal? Why'd you pick spending a summer in this fake reality selling people sugar with a side of escapism?"

"I'm starting college this fall, studying hospitality management, and I wanted to get a head start on earning my college work credits..." I rambled on about the hotel school and how the credits would give me the freedom to try other industries and jobs in later years.

"Anyone ever tell you you're kind of intense? Most people are just here to make some money and party all summer," Tory cut me off.

"Oh," I looked down at the pink t-shirt in my hands, all hopes of belonging slipping away.

"Don't worry—I'll show you how to live a little this summer," she smiled coyly, but I could tell she really meant it.

She was tough, or at least pretending to be, and I decided to be grateful to have her in my corner. And my room.

"Thanks," I smiled back while making a silent wish that her idea of living a little wouldn't be too far off from a nice bike ride around the island followed by a big scoop of ice cream overlooking the lake.

———

AFTER TAKING A HOT SHOWER—AND checking that the duct tape was indeed still intact—I crawled into my bed. I had told my mom a quilt would be too thick for summer, but, as always, she was right. Despite the beautiful day, it was freezing out.

I laid back on my single pillow, fidgeting beneath my quilt, and tried to clear my mind. This time of night was always when it was the loudest, even on the most mundane of days, but tomorrow would be a big day, too. I needed to sleep well, even if this was a new place with a stranger sleeping about three feet away from me. Tory had taken an 'all-natural sleeping pill' and was snoring softly in the bed beside mine with a diffuser humming faintly while it dispersed a lavender mist into the air.

I may have been here to get ahead on my college work credits, but this summer was going to prepare me for college in more ways than one.

I made a silent wish that I could handle it.

THREE

Mackinac Island Travel Tip #3:
Only buy fudge that's molded directly on a marble table.
If you want oven-baked fudge, make it at home.

THERE WAS something about the way the screen door squeaked and slammed as I entered the fudge shop that instantly took me back to summer camp. The shop was old, cozy, and filled with laughter, just like my camp bunk. The butterflies swirling in my stomach calmed as they remembered the feeling of previous summers spent in the mainland of northern Michigan, a warm nostalgia taking their place in my belly.

Before the screen door fully slammed, I was encapsulated by a sugary sweet stickiness that clung to my skin instantly. It was both overwhelming and the best smell I had ever encountered at the same time.

I could do this. Sure, it was my first day having a real, stable job, and I had never worked an eight-hour shift before, but it felt familiar. The shop calmed my nerves.

The intimidation I had felt at the apartment was replaced

by an ease of knowing that work was something I could master. This was what I was here for, I reminded myself. Give me a task, and I will complete it with excellence.

"You must be Ariella Abrams! Right on time," a voice materialized from behind the counter. "I'm Violet, the manager of this shop, the one down the road and the one in Mackinaw City. You'll mostly be working in this shop, which is great since you live upstairs. Are you ready for a tour?"

Before I could answer, the gruff woman was marching off past the antique wooden display cases of saltwater taffy and peanut brittle into the back room, and I figured I should try my best to keep up. The store had a black and white checkered tile floor with olive green accents on the walls. It was dated but welcoming. The back room, on the other hand, was all stainless steel, stark white, and chaotically filled with shipping boxes.

"This is where we store all the extra supplies. You see this milk? We use real milk, none of that powdered stuff. That's why our fudge is better than everyone else's on the island. Here. This is where you will clock in each day," she grabbed a piece of paper with my name on it and messily wrote the time in loopy blue ink. "Don't forget to clock out when you go on break and finish up. Understood?"

"Sounds good," I confirmed that I was keeping up with her rapid-fire tour.

"This door connects to the kitchen with your meals and the stairs to your apartment. Employee meals are offered for lunch and dinner, Monday to Friday, most weeks, and on the weekends there is stuff for you to heat up in the freezers."

This industrial kitchen looked like it was made for cooking, and I was relieved that I would indeed not be expected to cook for myself upstairs. The apartment kitchen was used exclusively for its ability to keep drinks cold and convenient.

"Back through here is the candy room. It has a window

out to the main floor so people can see that we make all the truffles and turtles right here onsite."

"Wow."

Willy Wonka's chocolate factory had nothing on this place. The candy room had glass drawers lining the walls with rainbows of sprinkles, different shades of chocolates, and a wide array of horse carriage and bike-shaped molds. The chocolatier was currently filling a flower mold with rich dark chocolate and offered a partial salute of acknowledgment in my direction.

"Some of the other stores ship their chocolates in, only making their fudge onsite. We aim to keep everything crafted in-house. Through here, you arrive back out front. The guys take care of most of the work when it comes to fudge making, but you might be asked to pitch in here or there with pouring or molding if we are really busy."

"Sounds good," I chimed in so she knew I was still following along.

"And this. This is the fudge counter. You'll spend most of your time back here. The real crowds don't start until next week, so this week we will show you the ropes. It's pretty simple, but it gets busy fast. We have boxes back here pre-folded for one, three, and five fudge slices. Anytime that you aren't helping a customer, you should be folding boxes so they are ready for the next rush. Any questions?"

I had barely had time to keep up, too distracted by the marble fudge tables and copper cauldron boiling over an open flame to have formed any coherent questions.

"No? Great. This is Emma," she gestured to a girl standing behind the counter who was organizing fudge slices in the display that ran the entire length of the shop. She was about my age with wavy auburn hair, her face and arms speckled with freckles. "She is working here this summer on a visa from Wales and can show you the ropes."

Concluding the tour and my formal training, she headed to the candy room, leaving us alone in the shop. Looking around, I tried desperately to remember everything I had just seen and heard.

"Hi, it's so nice to meet you," Emma gave a knowing smile. "I just started last week. I know it seems like a lot, but you will have the hang of it in no time. Violet is the best and spends most of her time at this location, so we really lucked out being placed here."

"That's good to know. I might be suffering low-grade whiplash from that tour," I chuckled. "I'm Ariella, but you can call me Ella. Are you living in one of the apartments upstairs, too?"

"No, down the street at the Purple House." Her accent was sweet, just like her demeanor.

"Awesome. How'd you decide to come here for the summer? I've never been, and I'm only from a few hours away."

"My uni arranges for people to come work on the island each summer, and one of my friends did it last year. I was incredibly jealous of her stories, so naturally, I had to sign up to come this year."

"That's awesome!" I shifted my weight from foot to foot.

Was there a group that had all come together for the summer? Would I be the only new person this summer who came to the island alone?

"You're from nearby?"

"Compared to you, yes. Ann Arbor. My parents work for the university there, so I've lived in Michigan all my li—"

I was cut off by a now familiar voice.

"Ladies. If you have time to lean, you have time to clean. At least wipe down the counters while you're chatting," Violet raised her eyebrows as a friendly smirk spread across her face to indicate this was part of our training, and she wasn't actually upset that we were chatting on the job.

For the rest of the day, I shadowed Emma, starting with a tasting of every flavor of fudge on the line. By the fifth flavor, my cheeks were flushed from sugar, and my taste buds danced around my mouth. Each flavor was better than the last, melting on my tongue with bliss. I started taking smaller and smaller bites as I worked my way down the counter, but by the time I placed a chunk of dark chocolate sea salt caramel in my mouth, I fully understood why people traveled near and far to this undoubtedly secluded destination. The fudge was worth the journey, no matter the length. Between the dark chocolate sea salt caramel, chocolate peanut butter, and chocolate orange, I couldn't pick just one favorite.

After that Emma taught me how to fold boxes, pack orders, and process payments. Our preference was cash, but we had a single card reader that took about 45 seconds to process. It sounds short, but when a family of five is waiting for fudge, it is a lifetime.

In the afternoon, I met Marlani. She had worked at Rosanna's for the last five summers. She has a husband and a son back home in Jamaica, but, since this is the off-season for tourism there, she works and lives on the island to save up for the winter. Then in the winter, her husband works locally in Jamaica.

I could tell she was no-nonsense, and I respected her sensibility immediately. She showed me how to scoop ice cream, which was way harder than it looked, and how to pack the waffle cones without causing them to crack in my hand. Two cones were sacrificed in the training. Based on first impressions alone, it was obvious she carried a lot of the weight around here, a regular who came back every summer and knew how to do things with the utmost efficiency.

Breaks were staggered, but I took my 30 minutes out back

on the dock for lunch. The break dock was private to our building and extended about 15 feet into the water. There were two picnic tables and a few small boats that tapped into the wooden dock with a steady pattern on either side. Even from this far out on the dock, I could smell the sweet mixture of cream and cocoa wafting out of the back of the shop. It was the dreamiest break room I could imagine.

Taking full advantage of my break, I popped upstairs to grab a band-aid for the blister that had been forming on the back of my foot. Opening the ever-unlocked door, I was surprised to find a tall girl in the middle of moving in.

"Hey! I'm Veronica. You must be one of my roommates."

"Hey, I'm Ariella, but you can call me Ella. I moved in yesterday and work downstairs," I slowed my frantic pace and acted unaffected by her presence as if it wasn't weird at all to be greeted by strangers in the place you lived.

"No way! I am working at the Rosanna's down the street for the second summer in a row. I am so pumped we are staying here. You really can't beat this view," she waved toward the living room and out to the lake that was shimmering in the afternoon sun.

"Incredible. I have to get back downstairs, but hopefully, we can catch up later?" I ran back down the stairwell, eager to not be late, and forgoing my much-needed band-aid.

FOUR

Mackinac Island Travel Tip #4:
Be open to making new friends.

AFTER EIGHT IMPOSSIBLY LONG hours on my feet, Emma invited me back to her house to see where some of the other people we worked with were living. Mackinac Island is pretty much a two-street town: Main Street and Market Street. Anywhere else is 'outside of the heart of downtown,' even if it's a stone's throw away. Emma's house was just a little way outside of the main town—less than three minutes by bike— and was a monstrous three-story house the color of a ripe plum. The color and wood details around each window were whimsical and the whole thing looked like it had been taken out of the pages of a children's book.

The house stood on the side opposite the street of the water, but there was still a view from the front porch which was filled with assorted wicker furniture. It was prime real estate, worthy of being a hotel or inn for paying customers, and I again found myself in disbelief that we all got to live here. There were two rows of bike racks to the side of the house where we discarded our bikes before heading up the white porch steps and into the living room. The house was unlocked, but it didn't seem like anyone was home.

Was this island run predominantly on trust?

"More people will be by later. I think everyone is just really getting started working today, so we are probably the first ones done," Emma glanced down at her smartwatch which flashed 6 PM through its neon pink background. "Oh, I closed my rings and spent ten hours standing today!"

If the blister throbbing on my heel was any indication, the novelty of that would wear off quickly. We chatted effortlessly, getting to know each other better with each passing moment. I learned that Emma was studying hospitality as well and hoped to travel the world working in luxury resort towns. This was the first stop on her world tour and her first time traveling outside of the UK and Europe. She was positively thrilled to be here and was planning to spend next summer working on a vineyard in South America.

Her casual outfit and the way she leaned back on the couch gave her this carefree '*I don't know how pretty I am*' look that I couldn't help but notice with a tinge of jealousy. She had a great sense of humor and an overall calm presence. At only two years older than me, she was the youngest person I had met so far, but I still instantly looked up to her. By the time the door swung open to start the party an hour later, we were both laughing hysterically, cheeks tight from smiling so big.

"Hello, hello!" Andrc walked in with arms full of bags. "Who's ready for a party? I invited all the guys from Donnie's and Tory promised she'd stop by with the group from the Inn."

I had been invited to parties in high school, but always preferred going to the mall or watching a movie with my friends. I wasn't sure if I was really the party type, but after two days of finding myself inadvertently at parties, I would need to change that if I wanted a social life this summer.

Growing up in a big ten college town, you have ample opportunities to go out, even outside of the typical high school parties. This is especially true if one of your siblings goes to the University of Michigan, and my big sister, Abigail, is going to be a senior this year. She was consistently trying to get me out of my shell to hang out with her on campus last year, but even that wasn't my scene.

There was one football Saturday when I didn't come up with a worthwhile excuse quick enough and had to agree to tailgate with her. My mom dropped me off at her house downtown around 10 AM, and the darty (day party) was already in full swing. Porches filled with maize and blue. Beer pong tables set up in front lawns. Random plastic fences lining yards gave the illusion of separation from the sidewalks and any passersby.

Abigail had always been incredibly social, quick to make friends, and easygoing in every conversation. She had large groups of friends and was constantly going to parties in high school, never opting to go to the mall or watch a movie instead. In many ways, Emma reminded me of her. Nevertheless, Abigail had always accepted that I was more interested in books, shopping, and makeup than sports and Ann Arbor's social scene and respected my boundaries.

Until that day. That day, my big sister woke up and clearly decided I needed to get out of my own way before starting college myself, and she knew I would be safer doing it with her than anyone else.

After introducing me to all her friends, we walked a few blocks from her college house and past a bouncer (yes, tailgates have bouncers in Ann Arbor) and into a backyard. The yard was filled with hundreds of people and a DJ. Abigail knew everyone and before I could process what was happening, we were asked by a fratty-looking boy in a blue basketball jersey to do an ice luge.

An ice luge is exactly what it sounds like—a giant ice sculpture in the shape of a slide with a spot at the bottom where you put your mouth directly on the ice. The boy asked if we wanted raspberry or strawberry lemonade and then yelled to get down.

Mimicking my big sister as I so often had, I dropped down on my knees in the cold, mushy grass and put my mouth on the base of the ice. I must have subconsciously nodded 'yes' to strawberry lemonade and without clear warning, a stream of ice-cold vodka was cascading into my mouth.

What felt like minutes went by without it stopping. I was panicking as to what to do before I finally realized I had to just get up off the grass for it to stop. There were plenty of vodka bottles so no one was worried about wasting or spilling on me, and they would keep it flowing as long as I would allow.

People cheered as I got up and wiped the dripping vodka from my chin—I had accidentally set the record for the day. For the first time in my life, I belonged at the party. I was no longer watching from the party sidelines, imagining what it would be like to be that carefree, and to be honest, I did like it. It was exhilarating, and I was surprisingly proud of my record despite not usually having a competitive edge.

The rest of the day was a blur, but somewhere around game time—2 PM—my mom picked me up and took me to Noodles & Company for a big bowl of buttered noodles. We then wandered to Michael's craft store, and I aimlessly tried to keep my cool, filling the shopping cart with spools of yarn that would inevitably never be used and end up in the craft supply graveyard in our basement storage room for decades to come.

While I hadn't chased that feeling, I couldn't deny that I thought about it often. Wondered even if there was an alternate universe out there where that was my life every weekend.

But no one knew me here, and this could be that alternate universe.

I wasn't the girlie girl who stuck to her friends and her books. The girl who didn't like sports even though she lived in a town whose weekend entertainment was built entirely on collegiate sports and how fast athletic teenagers could run while still hungover from the night before. I knew I was a fish out of water, but that didn't mean I couldn't find my way into the lake. I could be someone people not only wanted at the party but also expected to find in the center of the room.

I grabbed a spiked seltzer and joined the group dancing in the living room.

FIVE

**Mackinac Island Travel Tip #5:
Ask people where they are visiting from. The answers
might surprise you.**

WE WENT BACK to Emma's, the Purple House, the next night after work. A few more people had moved in today, filling all 16 beds in the house, and everyone said there was going to be a crowd tonight.

Emma and I sat up on a gray woven couch that had seen better days in the main living room. Before we even made a dent in our seltzers, Emma was whisked away to meet someone who was doing the same work exchange program as her, and I was alone. I scanned the room for someone I knew and could talk to. Where were my roommates? Shouldn't Chase and Andre be here by now? Or even Veronica?

"Hey, I'm George," a guy with a British accent so thick that it sounded fake and the dreamiest brown hair—you know the type that flops effortlessly into perfect waves without looking greasy with product—plopped down on the couch next to me.

He had a soft, crooked smile with a dimple on only one side and striking hazel eyes. He was wearing a nicer-than-average gray henley shirt with a few buttons on it, sleek black shorts, and white sneakers. He was on the shorter end but stood confidently in a way where I wouldn't have even noticed if not for my staring.

"I'm Ella. Where are you working this summer?"

Trying to mask the fact that I had just fallen in love with this stranger, I averted my eyes, fidgeting with the friendship bracelet on my wrist and carefully inspecting my own white Puma sneakers. I counted ten scuffs that had appeared on my shoes since arriving on the island, making a mental note to clean them when I got back to the apartment.

"Donnie's. Just started today, but I can already tell it's going to be brilliant. A true American summer."

Hmm, so the accent was real. My pulse quickened as I ran my fingers through my dark brown hair, hoping the waves were looking more effortless and less messy than usual. Had I remembered to wear mascara today? I lightly touched a lash to confirm.

"That's awesome. I am at Rosanna's next door to Donnie's," I stumbled over my words, seeking ways to keep the conversation going.

Had I blinked since he sat down? Luckily, while I forced my eyes to blink at an unnatural beat, we were interrupted by the dazzling duo that is Chase and Andre.

They were starting a game of flip-cup in the middle of the living room. Andre was fighting a gray folding table into the upright and locked position while Chase gathered the players off the couches, convincing all 12 of us to drop our conversations and get in on the game

"The game is easy. It's a relay between both sides of the table. Everyone has a cup of beer and as soon as the person to your side successfully chugs and flips the cup from right side up to upside down, you go. And so on until the last person," Chase swiftly brought me up to speed on the rules while demoing the flip of a cup on the edge of the table. "You and George can start us off. Stand here."

I moved into position at the end of the table crossing my fingers beneath the table in hopes that I understood the all-too-simple rules.

"Don't worry. I haven't played before either," George smiled from across the plastic folding table that was coated in dried beer from who knows when as we gently placed our red cups in front of us.

They were generously filled with a bubbling light beer we would be expected to chug at the start of our turns.

"Down, up, down," the group chanted as we kicked off the game, and I locked eyes with George for the first time.

Flipping as fast as I could, my cup was flying everywhere, my quivery hands unable to make a stable motion.

"Gentle!" someone I hadn't met yet hollered from down my side of the table.

Finally thriving under pressure, I tried again, flicking the base of the cup gently, it flew up before landing perfectly upside down in front of me. The guy on my left went next, hustling to make up for my slow start before the game continued its way down the row. Somehow my team managed to catch up with the last person.

"I guess you win. Want to grab some fresh air?" George asked.

I nodded my head, not wanting to risk saying the wrong thing and changing his mind. Of everyone here, why did he want to hang out with me? We made our way out to the big front porch, sitting down on the wooden steps overlooking the lake. The road was deserted at this hour, giving us a clear view across the street to the calm water, shining still in the moonlight of the harbor.

"So where are you from?"

I was guessing London by his accent, but I had only met a handful of people in the UK and didn't want to embarrass myself if he was actually from somewhere else.

"London."

I was right.

"Awesome. I've always wanted to visit. Do you live in the city or is it like New York where everyone says they are from there even if they live two hours away?"

His laugh was infectious, easing my nerves until I felt so comfortable that I forgot how uneasy I was supposed to feel in this type of situation.

"I am indeed from London-London," he said and smiled. Damn, I loved his crooked smile. "I'm studying economics there, and my family thought a summer in America would be good for me. I've been to New York City before—the actual city not two hours away—but this is my first time in the Midwest."

"I've always wanted to go to London."

"It's like everywhere else—seems dreamy if you've never been, but actually rather average if you're from there. Like any other city."

"Have you been to Detroit? Or even Chicago?" I laughed. "I'm guessing London is pretty different."

"We all romanticize the unknown."

His dimple settled on his face, his soft voice trailing off in the night. There was a long list of things I was romanticizing, but I couldn't help but wonder what other unknowns someone like him could be musing about.

"I suppose so."

My eyes met his under the dim porch lights. The candor of the moment continued as he told me more about his home and his travels. I mentally took notes on everything, filing each detail into my brain, not wanting to forget a single thing about him.

Our conversation was cut off as some others joined us in the brisk night air, and unlike earlier there was a flare of disappointment in the pit of my stomach as the moment was broken. Unsure what else to do, I tried to meet as many people as possible. There was Sophie, who I'd briefly met my first night who was rooming with Emma, Jack who went to Central Michigan and would be working at Donnie's, Mike who grew up on the island and was at the Inn with Tory, and the list went on. It was going to be a miracle if I could match the right names, faces, and jobs the next time I saw people.

Overall, it was quite a motley crew with a mix of people working here out of necessity for a decent summer job, and people on break from college, many of whom were quite wealthy and doing this for a good story. I was surprised how many had come all the way here from abroad, seeking an excuse to spend the summer in the States. Regardless of everyone's differences or what factors initially drew them to the island, there was a vibe in that air that made me confident we would all get along quite well.

As I drifted to sleep in my twin bed, covers pulled tight to my nose, I thought about the one face that I knew I wouldn't be forgetting overnight.

George.

SIX

Mackinac Island Travel Tip #6:
The fudge is great, but make sure to try the other sweet treats, too.

THE NEXT DAY, I woke up to the sound of a slamming dresser drawer. Tory had the 7 AM shift at the Inn, but I wasn't working until 3 PM. My back and legs were sore from so much standing the past two days and, after getting back to the apartment so late last night, all I wanted to do was stay in bed.

Sadly, I was a terrible sleeper and once I was up, I was up. Knowing I would fail any attempts to go back to sleep, I peeled myself out of bed to make the most of my morning. I still had not biked all the way around the island, and it was at the top of my to-do list.

Stretching out my leg cramps from the long days stationed on the old tile floors of the fudge shop, I threw on some black cropped leggings and a pink t-shirt before grabbing my bike from the rusted racks behind our apartment building, pausing briefly to take in the view of the lake. At home, my view consisted of a handful of trees and my neighbor's back porch, windows so close together you had to be mindful not to look in. Here, the water was still, glistening in the sun and stretching as far as I could see, with no desire or need to avert my eyes. I couldn't believe I actually got to live here.

As my bike tires rolled round and round on the smooth pavement of the trail around the island, my mind indulged itself in memories of the night before. Replaying my conversation with George, I thought about how certain he was in his future. The easy way with which he laughed at my jokes. No one had ever called me funny before, but being with him had made me feel clever. He was unlike anyone I had met before—self-assured, confident, and still kind. It was a combination unheard of in my stratosphere of American high schools.

I wondered if he was thinking about me, too. Ever the hopeless romantic, I pictured him at work, thinking back on the same conversion right now. As my tires rolled on, I became more convinced that he was. I couldn't possibly have been the only one to feel that spark.

By the time 3 PM rolled around, I was ready to go back to work. I pulled on my uniform—an olive green polo and khakis —and ran down the stairs for the world's shortest commute. Clocking in, there was a renewed bounce to each step I took.

It was only day three, but I was already getting the hang of it. My eyes were animated as I recommended fudge flavors to each family, having tasted them all and feeling confident in my suggestions. When they asked to sample five different flavors, I knew what order to give them in to limit the amount of dancing around required behind the counter. I even knew the mental math for the taxes on each of the typical packages. Two new girls had joined the team today, and I beamed as I taught them the ropes—already an old pro.

The hours ticked by, and the fudge shop transformed before me. Early afternoon was busy before a lull around dinner time and then when the sun set for the evening we had another rush for the late-night ice cream eaters before it slowed again. The fudge makers always finished making their last slabs of fudge for the night during the dinner time lull, and cleaned up, leaving their stations ready to begin fresh tomorrow.

"Ella, do you want to learn how to clean the popcorn machine tonight?" Marlani, my coworker from Jamaica whom I had already grown fond of, summoned me from behind the counter.

She looked so small, standing on her toes and trying to reach the top of the red and white vintage popcorn machine.

"Yeah, that'd be great." Eager to make myself useful, I ran around the back of the counter toward her.

"First, take all this leftover popcorn and lay it on the fudge tables. Someone will come in later to coat it in caramel to sell tomorrow. Then, the hard part starts."

I carefully emptied the machine, trying to avoid the sticky kettle that was still hot from its own long day of work.

"The key to a clean machine is doing it multiple times. Some of the girls just give it a quick wipe, but then you get all these streaks in the front window. I hate streaks. It looks messy and unsanitary, so I am going to teach you the right way. Dump this little tray of kernels, then grab this bucket and use warm water and dish soap. For this part, we can use a regular rag."

Marlani started on the machine, getting up on her tiptoes to get the front corners and wiping down the kettle.

"Now, I will let you in on my secret. After most of the butter and visible dirt is gone, I take some Windex—it's food safe—don't worry, and a newspaper. The newspaper doesn't leave streaks the same way paper towels do, so you want to do this on the outside. Go around the front and finish it for me."

I crumpled the paper and wiped it away, polishing the

glass. We were using a newspaper to clean a popcorn machine —and it was actually working.

After the popcorn adventure, Marlani taught me how to use a large metal paddle to scrape up the excess fudge people dropped on the floors of the shop and how to mix the perfect mopping solution. She hummed the song *Closing Time* by Semisonic while we worked, a lemony fresh scent filling the air, and never complained about how much there was to do or how it was already well past the end of our shifts.

I followed her lead in counting out the cash in the drawers and then, our boss, Inez showed up. Three families own most of the businesses on Mackinac Island, and hers is one of them.

"Ella! So good to finally meet you! I see you're in the best possible hands learning from Marlani. She has been a part of our family for ages and is the best of the best. How'd it go today?"

This was my first time meeting her in person, and I was a bit surprised at just how approachable she was. Between her unassuming sweatshirt and easygoing smile, I had to look twice to be sure it was her. It was though, and I realized she was also the woman in the photos of Violet in the back office —the two of them in their teen years, embraced over the fudge table.

"Great day. Here's all the cash and receipts from the cards."

Before I could respond, Marlani passed Inez a large beige sack of everything we had meticulously tallied.

"Thank you. Ella, how's the apartment?" she asked.

"It's great! Thank you so much. I feel so lucky to be living right here on Main Street."

Should I ask her about shadowing Tory? No one has mentioned me working in the hotels yet, but I also don't want to bother her. Especially our first time truly meeting. Shadowing at the Inn was the goal, my ticket to earning my college work credits before school even started, but making a good impression on Inez was the first step.

"It really is magical, isn't it?" Inez's gaze wandered around the shop with a sense of pride and pure happiness that made all the hard work feel worthwhile. "We help people make some of their best, lifelong memories on this island. My family has lived here my whole life. We started with this shop, and now have four fudge shops, three hotels, three clothing and gift shops, and four restaurants. There is honestly nowhere else I'd like to live. Although, if you ask me in January I might say otherwise!"

Inez's eyes glistened under the fluorescent lights, clearly grateful for the legacy and impact her family had on this magical place.

I hoped my life's work would one day leave a similar imprint on people.

"Very fair! I love it here already though. Thanks again for taking a chance on me and giving me this opportunity. I can tell it will be an amazing summer," I stiffened my posture, hoping I was making a good impression.

I had only spoken to Inez twice before—once when she called me to ask a couple of questions after I had submitted a resume and cover letter online, and again when she called to offer me the position. My original application had been for the Inn, but given my lack of any real experience, she could only offer me the fudge shop with a chance to learn at the Inn. I was grateful and determined to make the most of it. Plus, any hours at the Inn would put me ahead for the next four years. It was weird though that she hadn't mentioned it at all. Maybe she thought I was too busy working here?

"By the way, I completely forgot. I will set up some time for you to shadow Tory at the Inn soon. We need you over here, but I'm sure Violet can spare you for one or two days this summer to see how the Inn operates."

One. Or. Two. Days. ONE OR TWO DAYS?

I was hardly going to be working at the Inn. I would barely get any credits for college. This summer was not going to set me up for fall at all.

"That would be great," I choked out, masking my disappointment and scrambling my brain for how to fix this.

Nothing came to mind.

"Glad to hear that. Well, I will be seeing you soon, but don't be shy to pop by my house if you need anything. I live two doors down from the big purple house and am usually on my front porch."

With that, Marlani and I finished our last few closing activities and clocked out for the evening. She was headed back to her house, a place she shared with the other island regulars every summer, and me to the Purple House with my new friends.

SEVEN

Mackinac Island Travel Tip #7:
Support as many small businesses as you can.

IF YOU'RE LOOKING for salty air on Mackinac Island... you won't find it on the lakefront beaches, but you will find it at Donnie's. The Bureau of Business has long blocked chain restaurants from opening here, so the island has Donnie's Burgers. Fast food made fresh and owned locally.

Andre mentioned that I could grab a bite there anytime I wanted, so I figured it was worth checking out on my first day off. Located right next door to Rosanna's, it's a mystery how the smells of salty, crisp fries and chicken nuggets never make their way through the clouds of chocolatey sugar that filled our shop.

"How's it going, Chase?"

The room was filled with deep maroon vinyl diner booths and, much like the rest of the island, it felt like it was from another era. The black and white checkered floors matched ours at the fudge shop, but the walls were covered in old posters of Island events from the 1900s—literal signs that Donnie's had been here through it all.

"Good, the morning rush just died down. I swear, if I never have to serve breakfast to demanding families on vacation again after this summer..." His voice trailed off as he ran around, wiping down all the empty tables.

I hadn't noticed when I first arrived, but most of them were covered in trash even though there were very clear trash bins to leave your trays near the exit.

"Yeah, it seems like people think just because you're working, you're not a real person. It's the same next door. Yesterday, someone even asked me to throw out their used tissue."

"Are you serious? That's disgusting!" Chase laughed.

"YUP. I was so flustered that I said yes, and then I was suddenly holding a snotty tissue behind the fudge counter," I shook my head, still in disbelief. "Pretty sure that's against the health code."

"The real issue is the kids. They call off ten things they want, and just as I am entering them in, the parents snap back to reality and ask for it to be taken off the bill. Like no, sorry it is not my fault your kids don't know what they are allowed to have," Chase finished the last of the tables and circled back to the register. "Anyway, everyone else is on break so it's up to me to get everything spotless before the masses come back to destroy it during lunch. Can I get my favorite roomie anything?"

"Is there anything you have leftover from breakfast you need to get rid of?"

Based on the state of the overflowing trash cans, it was clearly a brutal morning, and the last thing I wanted to do was add to the list of demands Chase had dealt with today.

"Yes, but I'm not giving you that trash. I will make you something fresh-ish."

Laughing at his own joke, Chase gestured toward the kitchen to signal that anything I wanted could be mine.

"If you're sure... I would love some fries."

"That's all?" he tilted his head and widened his eyes, as if not fully convinced.

"Yeah, I am going to bike around the island and have a proper lunch later."

I was dying to try the chicken nuggets, but I felt like it was too much to ask. It wasn't as if I would be unwilling to get him a box of fudge or as many scoops of ice cream as he wanted, but I was still reluctant to be a burden.

"Alright, then your wish is my command. Be back in a sec!"

A few minutes later, I was sitting on the break dock with a brown bag full of piping hot french fries so drenched in salt that I had somehow finished my Donnie's XL diet coke before the fries. They were perfect, and I was glad that I was too self-conscious to go back there daily, otherwise, this was going to become a habit.

I spent the rest of my day off biking around the island. Starting by taking the 8.2-mile journey that is M-185 around the perimeter of the island, my hands gripped tightly on my handlcbars, body hunched over, as I sped across the road, practically floating along the water's edge. Something about the crisp, fresh air blowing on my face and billowing my long brown hair beneath my helmet mixed with the feeling of being alone cast an umbrella of zen. It was just me, and my thoughts.

I allowed my mind to wander, thinking of all the 'what-ifs' and adventures the summer had in store. By mile seven, I had mentally planned numerous outings that I was knowingly not fearless enough to take. My mind exploring the corners of my wildest dreams, I began to ride uphill into the woods. Once you're off the main loop, the island is a series of unpaved trails that cross around seemingly endlessly.

I biked for hours, working off all the fudge I had tasted these first few days, and then meandered around the town, going in and out of t-shirt shops and boutiques. Having cataloged all the shops, including making note of which were selling the same clothes at different prices, I felt at a loss for what to do next. Most activities on the island were designed for tourists, meaning they are best done in groups and cost more money than I had. This island was designed for Paris in season one of *Gilmore Girls*, and season six Paris had no place here. It was a town comprised of both the haves and the have-nots. You could either afford to partake in the lures of Main Street or you could spend your time behind a desk, creating memorable moments for the fortunate vacationers.

But what would be my plans for future days off? Was I actually so uncreative that I couldn't think of anything else to do on my first day? Would my off days ever line up with Emma? I guessed that because I met all my friends at work, that was somewhat unlikely, and I would need to learn how to enjoy doing things alone. If only my aversion to relaxing would take a break...

Not ready to admit defeat, I took me, myself, and my empty wallet on another ride through some houses at the edge of town. Just as I was enjoying myself, it started to rain, forcing me back to the big apartment.

"Figures," I grumbled under my breath as I pulled open the door and ditched my soggy sneakers.

"Ella, you don't have fenders on your bike, do you?" Andre was flopped on the couch, still in his maroon Donnie's uniform.

"What are fenders?" A red flush slowly crept its way onto my face, as if my body knew my mistake before my mind.

Andre erupted into laughter, "Covers for your bike tires," he choked out through a fit of tears.

"Okay... and how do you know I don't have those by looking at me?"

If there is one thing I was confident of at this moment, it was that my cheeks were now fully beet red.

"You can tell who has them every time it rains..." He regained his composure before adding, "Check out your back in the mirror. You're going to want to do some laundry."

Sure enough, my back had a line going straight up from my butt to my shoulders. It looked like mud, but even in the short time I had been here, I knew it was more than that. I had a splattered mixture of mud and horseshit all up my back.

"Anyway, some people are going to come over later. Want to see if Emma or any of the others want to hang?"

"Bet. I'll text her now."

My cheeks still red, I slinked off to the bathroom to change as quickly as possible. Sticky with sweat and other unmentionables, I checked the duct tape, not willing to bear further embarrassment today, and turned on the shower. How was I supposed to know that this would happen? My old bike had never been taken out in the rain before.

"Stupid island. Stupid horse. Stupid bike. Stupid job," I muttered under the scalding hot shower.

Nothing was going the way I planned.

I flopped on the bed and scrolled through my social media feeds for the first time in days to delay going into the living room and evade further ridicule by giving Andre time to forget the image of my poop-covered back. And to give me time to stop being such a complete grump.

I could still turn this day around. Andre said the guys were coming, which likely included George, and I really wanted to figure out where this was heading. If he showed up and only talked to me, that would be the confirmation I was looking for that he was at least on the path to being as interested as I was.

Tonight, I would focus on George.

Tomorrow, I would buy some fenders.

———

PEOPLE TRICKLED INTO THE APARTMENT, some in work clothes and others changed to go to bars later in the night.

"Ariella, can I make you a drink?" Chase had stocked up on the finest the grocery store had to offer in our price range, meaning bottom-shelf booze and assorted pops.

"Sure, whatever you're having."

I had strategically avoided having anything other than seltzer all week, slowly sipping on one can per evening, but I figured Chase wasn't the type to make anything too strong for me. As long as he didn't have an ice luge, I would be able to handle whatever he concocted.

I spent the next hour with Andre, detailing our respective dating histories. He and his boyfriend of four years had recently broken up, and he was looking for a summer fling to move on. Mike, who had lived on the island his whole life, had caught his attention, and Andre was hoping to feel out his availability tonight. Andre and I could not have been more different. He was in his mid-20s. I was barely a day over 18. He was Black. I was White. He was gay. I was straight. He was confident and knew people noticed him the second he walked into a room, and I was lodged somewhere between blending into the wallpaper and offering to take coats upon entry—visible, but not memorable.

Tonight, we were exactly the same.

Both hopelessly stood up by people who didn't even know we were waiting for them.

Shrinking back into the crook of the couch, I tried to suppress just how affected I was by his absence. Had I miscalculated George's interest the other night? The buzz of all the new friends I had made in the past few days was deflated by the disappointment of waiting around for him, of longing for the satisfying ease I had felt the other night.

With the energy winding down at the big apartment for the night, Andre and the rest of the 21 and up crowd headed out to one of the cheaper bars on Main Street. Luckily for me, Emma was still a few weeks away from her birthday and hung back to keep me company.

We snacked on some leftover chicken nuggets and fries that one of the guys had brought up after closing Donnie's (the nuggets were as good as I imagined) and gossiped.

"I wish we had some ice cream," I said through mouthfuls of salty snacks.

"Ew. Are you one of those salty and sweet girls?"

"Yes! Are you not?" my eyes widened in disbelief.

"Not even a little. The combination of sweet and salty is repulsive," she shook her head in disgust. "Honestly, I am surprised it doesn't smell worse up here with Donnie's and Rosanna's mixing in the air."

"As someone who has to sleep here, I am very thankful for that."

"Anyway, enough about snacks. Who do you think is the cutest?" she redirected us.

"George... What about you?" I crossed my fingers behind my back, making a silent wish that we wouldn't both have the same taste.

"Chase. He is majorly cute, and I like his humor. It's a little off-putting, but sincere at the same time. Do you know what I mean?" My body jerked up on the couch, aggressively relieved that she was not interested in George. "George is a good choice though. I just didn't come here to date guys I could've met back home. You get full dibs there, just don't try sneaking into Chase and Andre's room in the middle of the night."

"I wouldn't even dream of it," I laughed, feeling lighter than I had in the past hour.

"So Tory is a little intense right?"

"A little?"

"A lot," Emma raised her eyebrows. "Do you sleep with one eye open?"

"Only every night," I mumbled under my breath, unsure just how much to admit Tory scared me. "But, I am going to stay on her good side. I think once you're in with her, you are in for life."

"Mhmm. That checks out," Emma grabbed another handful of the now soggy fries. "Veronica is chill though. I would hang out with her. Same with Sophie."

"Definitely," I agreed.

It was hard to imagine that a few days ago, we had never met. That I had been anxious about making new friends and worried about fitting in. Despite my earlier disappointments tonight, the outcome had been better. Emma was so down-to-earth, while also having a very confident cool girl vibe. The more time we spent together, the more she reminded me of my sister, Abigail. In a matter of a few nights, I officially had a friend that felt like home in my home away from home.

EIGHT

**Mackinac Island Travel Tip #8:
There are amazing restaurants on the island, and you
should try as many as you can.**

THE FIRST TWO weeks of working flashed by in a haze, with no real separation marking the start and end of each day. I had my routine down—work eight hours a day, six days a week at the fudge shop, and bike around the island on my day off. Each time Inez showed up during closing, she assured me that she would make good on our arrangement soon; but still, there had been no movement. I was growing antsy, but you know *patience is a virtue* and all that, so I put mine to the test. If I was patient enough, maybe I could prove myself valuable. Play the long game by not bothering anyone: A people-pleaser's guide to life.

Truthfully, my throbbing feet, burdened enough by my current workload, didn't mind the delay. Neither did my social life. I had big plans that weekend that would require every ounce of free time that I could muster.

On my first day of high school, someone with a sick

sense of humor put me in first-period gym class. That faithful Tuesday after Labor Day at 7:40 AM, I strolled into the gym which somehow reeked of sweat, even after a summer free of sprinting teens. I slowly shuffled my way to the green and yellow bleachers, my eyes scanning the crowd. I didn't recognize anyone from my middle school, so I sat down a little off to the side. Within a minute, a girl in a bright red matching workout set walked up to me and introduced herself as Mara. Ever since that day, she had been my best friend.

This weekend, Mara was going to come to visit me on the island, and my brain was vibrating with excitement about all the things I needed to show her and the people she needed to meet. She was going to love the Purple House and Emma. Of that, I was certain.

She would also meet George and assess the situation for me. Of where that was headed, I was less certain.

George and I had hung out a few more times at the Purple House this past week, and I was severely perplexed by him. Sometimes, he acted so interested that I couldn't imagine everyone else in the room couldn't see it. Other times, it felt like he wanted to be talking to anyone but me. And that was only counting the times he bothered to show up.

I really had a knack for getting myself into unrequited situationships. There was one boy in high school who I'd let drag me on for months. We studied together a bunch of times, often laying on our bellies side-by-side, I always sensed he was on the verge of asking me to go out, but it never went past studying on my purple shag rug. He was plenty smart himself, and I had finally come to terms with the fact that he wasn't pulling a Cady Heron and merely led me on to steal my notes.

Mara had helped me both see that and recover from the heartache he'd left behind. If the same thing was happening again, I needed her better judgment to get to this island.

49

Emma was great, but she was still too new of a friend to be anything other than unwaveringly supportive.

This situation called for the tough love that only a long-time best friend could provide.

———

AROUND NOON A FAMILY came into the shop. They were dressed head to toe in colorful biking gear, all swaying brightly-hued helmets around their wrists.

"I just love Mack-in-ack. Look how cute this shop is!" The woman in the group did a spin around the room, pausing to rest her hands on the waist-high white picket fence that separated the marble tables where the fudge was poured and molded from the rest of the room.

"Fudgies," Violet snorted under her breath as she walked behind me with a fresh batch of chocolate peanut butter fudge.

Us locals referred to anyone coming to the island solely to bike and buy fudge as fudgies. It was a lightly degrading word for tourists, and we even had a sign in the back room that read 'no fudgies allowed.' We didn't actually label specific people it often, usually it was just a generalized term for the masses of day trippers, but if someone was carrying a helmet and mispronouncing the name of the island, there was a fair chance someone would comment.

The island was named Mackinac Island and the town across the lake was Mackinaw City, but both were pronounced the same—Mack-in-aw. By my second day here I learned that people who came into the shop requesting Mack-in-ack fudge didn't understand that the island was named by the English who shortened the name by the French who incorrectly pronounced the original name given by the Native Americans.

And thus, the fudgie label was given with lots of love and appreciation for their patronage.

"Ella! We are so excited to be here. What should we get?" This particular fudgie was Mara's dad, and he was thrilled to see me.

"Hey! So happy you guys could make it. I will get you a box of my favorites. When did you get in?" I played my own personal game of Where's Waldo, searching the crowd in the shop for Mara before realizing she was on her phone pacing the sidewalk between Rosanna's and Donnie's.

"We took the 10 AM ferry. Mara has been complaining all morning that us waking her up at 6 AM to get here ruined her whole weekend, so seeing you will cheer her up. If she would just get off the phone..."

"Ella! This place is SO cute."

Right on cue, the screen door slammed as Mara wove her way through the crowd and over to my section of the counter. I perked up, waving her over to an empty spot across from me.

"I'm obsessed. Do you just eat fudge all day long? Seriously, I would."

"I definitely did the first week, but after that, you don't really want any of it," I chuckled and passed over the box of my five favorite slices.

My feet had never fully recovered from the blisters I formed those first few days. My legs were sore from standing. The fudge had become my frenemy. I still appreciated everything it had to offer the world, but I personally wanted nothing to do with it.

"Ugh, I don't think I would ever get sick of it," Mara practically drooled on the display case and my body tensed up, knowing it would be on me to clean up after her.

"When do you get off sweetie? We would love to take you to dinner," Mara's mom was kind and welcoming.

She always invited me over and treated me as part of the

family. Mara was an only child, and I was their honorary second daughter.

This past year, my parents were out of town the week of my birthday for my younger brother Jeremy's golf state championship. He was an amazing golfer, and the only Freshman to make the varsity team, so when they said we would have to postpone my birthday party, I completely understood. But Mara's parents refused to let me cancel, instead hosting at their house and decking out their basement for a slumber party with our closest friends. It will probably be my favorite birthday for the rest of my life.

"Around 6 PM, so that would be perfect. I can't wait to hear all about everything you have planned for your trip. Looks like you are going to do some serious biking today."

A pang of jealousy shot through me, wishing I could go out and enjoy the summer sun with them.

"Yes, they are dragging me to every 'must see' this island has listed online. They can't believe we have never been here," Mara rolled her eyes before spinning on her heels and letting the door slam shut behind her for the second time.

———

BY THE TIME 6 PM came around, I was sticky with sweat and wanted nothing more than to lie down. I couldn't do that though, so I quickly ran upstairs to the apartment for a two-minute shower and to change into a sundress. We were having dinner at a fancy restaurant on the far side of Main Street which required one of my best dresses. It was a Lilly Pulitzer shift I had thrifted online ahead of the summer, always prepared.

Running late, I zigzagged my way in and out of tourists on the sidewalk and down to meet Mara's family. The restaurant was in a quaint hotel with the main dining room around the back, situated directly on the waterfront. The decor was primarily pink and green patterns with nautical motifs scattered throughout.

"How was the day of exploration?" I joined them at the table, still catching my breath as I collapsed into my seat.

If I tried hard enough, my dress would camouflage me right into the patterned cloth booth.

"It was absolutely marvelous. This island is just too cute. I am so glad you gave us an excuse to finally make our way up here this summer!" Mara's mom gushed. "How's the job going? Everything you dreamed?"

"Honestly? I haven't started working at the Inn yet and don't know if it will really happen. The fudge shop is great, but I can only get college credits if I work over 50 hours in a hotel this summer. I don't want to be too pushy, but I also feel like if I was just going to work in a candy shop, I could've done that at home. Or worked at an Ann Arbor hotel for the whole summer," I rambled.

"Ellie, chill. You don't need the credits that bad. Just have fun. I'm missing out on having you at home this summer, so can you please act like it was worth it?" Mara poked my side. "Besides, home is boring. Credits or no credits this place is worth it."

I sucked in a deep breath, anxious about college and making sure the summer played its role in my larger life plan, but vowing to drop the topic for the rest of the meal, I took a large bite of my crab cakes. Mara was right—I had ditched her this summer and the least I could do was act gracious about it.

After dinner, Mara convinced her parents that she could sleep over at my apartment. I assumed my roommates wouldn't mind, given Tory had her boyfriend visit last weekend without asking me first, so we grabbed a couple of things from their hotel room and dropped them off before heading to the Purple House.

It was always a little random which nights would draw the biggest crowds at the Purple House or the big apartment. We didn't operate on the typical weekday/weekend schedule, but even as we were making our way up the uneven sidewalk to the porch, I could tell it would be a big night. Our group's unspoken plan-making seemed to be running at full throttle.

Based on the loud music and the vibrating wicker furniture that greeted us, I knew everyone would be there before I opened the ever-unlocked door. We almost had to push our way through the living room to get to Emma.

"Ella! Finally, you're here. George has been looking very lonely and just went out back. I think he was expecting you to be here tonight," Emma wrapped her arms around me in a loose hug while air-kissing my cheek in a way that I had come to expect.

"Really? I'll have to find him, but first—this is Mara. My best friend from home."

As anticipated, Emma and Mara instantly hit it off. Knowing they were in good company with each other, I shuffled my way through the crowd in search of George. We seldom went in the backyard, but if Emma saw him go this way, I would too.

"Look who decided to show up," a familiar voice called from above me, my heart pitter-pattered in my chest as I stepped into the yard to find him.

There he was. George was sitting on the awning of the porch, otherwise known as the roof, one story up.

"How'd you get up there?" I inspected the area for a ladder or some kind of garden trellis.

People always climbed trellises in the movies, right?

"Crawled out the window. This is me and Jack's room," he grinned his signature toothy smile.

"Nice," I nodded, pacing the yard while waiting for a proper invitation to join him.

"Yeah, it's a good place to think."

"Seems like it," I awkwardly bobbed my head, still hoping for an invitation.

"You want to come up?"

"You sure I won't get in the way of all your thinking?" I didn't wait for him to answer or change his mind, my stomach fluttering as I made my way back into the house.

"I'll meet you at the top of the stairs," George called after me.

True to his word, he met me at the top of the stairs before walking me through his shared room, which was just large enough to house two twin beds and a single dresser, and lifting me out the window and onto the rooftop.

"So why did you actually decide to come up here?" I settled in next to him, my bare legs scraping against the harsh, grainy roofing.

I ran my fingers along the back of my legs, subtly checking for blood while keeping a light smile on my face. That was going to leave a mark.

"Honestly? I just didn't want to play pong with Jack so I was hiding," he confessed.

"Have you played before?"

He paused. "Yes?" his voice went up as if questioning his own memory.

"So you haven't?" I teased.

"I have," he paused again, "but I'm rubbish at it."

"Sure," I shook my head, not believing for a second that that was true.

He was undoubtedly good at everything.

"So, what's your favorite thing in the world?" he turned to me, asking a lazy open-ended question that could have come from a deck of cards on conversation topics for people you don't actually want to talk to.

"Taylor Swift," just because the question was disingenuous, did not mean I had to give a fake answer.

"Taylor Swift?" George raised his eyebrows, his features just barely visible in the moonlight.

"Yes." Unlike him, I was fully confident in this statement.

"Why?"

"Pure talent. Glittery dresses. Easter eggs. Insane concert performances that are better than every Broadway show put together." He was silent, which I took as an invitation to continue. "It's the way she breaks the fourth wall. She doesn't act too cool or too famous to know what we, her fans, are doing. She loves and acknowledges us. We have an insane amount of inside jokes, and she references them directly to us at concerts and online. It's the way her life and mine could not be more different, yet I relate to every word of her songs. Honestly, the relationship I have with her is so pure and exactly how I would want all my friendships to be."

"Wow."

"I know, that was probably more than you were looking for."

I looked down at my white sneakers, lamenting my major oversharing of a monologue and counting the scuffs that had returned since I cleaned them a few days prior. Had I just passed up my opportunity to say something flirty with a rambling ode to Miss Swift? Would I have even known how to say something coy instead?

"Not at all. It's actually really cool. I know everyone is obsessed with her, but I never heard it laid out that way," he was carefully considering my words, having fully listened and trying to understand. "Play me one of your favorite songs. I want to hear."

"You want me to pick just one?" I laughed, pulling out my phone and clicking through Spotify. "Okay, so this one is exactly what I was talking about. She originally wrote it for her band back in 2010 when she thought she was writing her last album. It evolved though, and now it's her speaking to us, her fans, and telling us what a great run we've all had together."

I pressed play and George leaned his head back, closing his eyes to listen. I hadn't met many guys who were such good listeners. I watched him closely and waited for each small smile that graced his face at the cleverest lyrics.

"Why am I thinking about my best mate from growing up? I haven't spoken to him in years. I wonder what he's up to..." He was looking directly into my eyes, and I felt seen.

It was different from how I felt with my friends, who often understood the underlying meaning of my meandering stories based on their years of experience with them. It clicked in a way I always imagined it would when I met *the oh-so-ominous one*.

"You get it."

It was official. The best way to tell if a guy is going to treat you right is to explain your love of Taylor Swift to him. If he can listen and understand her, he's perceptive enough to be good to you, too. If he can't, it's a red flag.

We were up there for an hour before I realized how much time had passed. I had pretty much ditched Mara as soon as we got to the party, and there was no way I was going to be a bad friend tonight—after she traveled all the way here to see me—even if George was finally on the same page as me.

"Want to go downstairs? My friend from home is visiting, and we can all hang out," I didn't want to leave, but I was slowly entering bad friend territory with each passing minute.

"I'm actually pretty tired. I will come to say hi, but then I am going to call it."

I audibly sighed. It was as if a switch had flipped and the past hour hadn't happened.

I knew tired. We were all tired. Imagine standing on your feet all day with hundreds of people asking you for something.

We all felt and experienced that version of tiredness daily. If he cared, he would rally and come spend the rest of the night with us.

Despite his off-comment, George did seem to put in a fair amount of effort. He asked Mara a bunch of questions about herself and tried to make his own good impression. He could have saved himself some energy if he realized that making a good impression in this situation was not going to take much. Mara was elated to meet George. I had been texting her about him the last couple of weeks, and she had been dying to meet him. Everything she knew and felt about him she had experienced secondhand through my rose-colored eyes, so she already liked him plenty. Even with her healthy dose of natural skepticism.

Around 1 AM, Mara, Emma, and I shuffled our way over to Island Slice Pizza. It was located in the center of town and was the only place to end a night like tonight.

I wasn't drunk, barely having sipped the drink I was handed when we arrived at the Purple House, but that didn't keep me from babbling away about everything I had kept neatly in a box since earlier that evening. With my dinner vow forgotten, I exploded. About how George couldn't give a clear read. About how I was never even going to get to work at the inn. About how I smelled sugar and fudge 20 to 24 hours every day. I complained about everything.

Fortunately, there are certain complaints you can make to your nearest and dearest.

To anyone else, you simply sound entitled.

NINE

Mackinac Island Travel Tip #9:
Don't expect your room to be ready if you arrive before check-in.

AS IF SHE heard my late-night gossip session, Inez strolled into the fudge shop at 10 AM the next day. I had just said goodbye to Mara before starting work and was not feeling like my best self after last night.

"Hi Inez, anything I can help you with today?" I straightened up, trying my hardest to appear professional.

"Yes, I want you to shadow at the Inn this week. Is Violet here so we can talk about scheduling?"

"She's in the back."

It was finally happening! I did a little happy dance behind the counter as she disappeared into the back room. About ten minutes later, she returned and quietly informed me that tomorrow I would be opening with Tory at the Inn.

The next morning the alarm buzzed at 6:40 AM. Usually, I would roll over, wrapping myself into my blanket like a burrito, and pretend not to hear Tory mulling about the room, but today I was getting up too.

Groggily, I rose from my bed, brushed my teeth, and threw on one of the only front desk-worthy outfits I had with me. I hadn't packed much that wasn't athletic wear, sundresses, or Khaki shorts to go with my fudge shop uniform, but there was no uniform for the front desk at the Inn, and I needed to dress business casual. I crossed my fingers that a sundress would be acceptable.

"I don't like to talk in the morning. Can you just watch?" Tory asked a question that I knew only had one right answer.

It was 7 AM, and we had just arrived at the front desk.

"Sure, totally. No worries," I twiddled my thumbs, taking in the stacks of paper and countless checklists behind the desk.

The hotel lobby was small but colorful. There was a large vase of lilacs on the front desk, and the space was cozy in an authentic way that I'm sure all Inns aim to be.

"I'll teach you stuff later," Tory promised as she turned her attention back to scrolling through her phone.

Being a resort town, there was limited action until 8 AM, but once it hit 8... things were busy.

I watched Tory check guests out on a computer older than me, tag their bags for whichever of the three ferry lines they had selected, and accept bags from incoming guests who arrived too early to check in, wanting to make the most of their days on the island.

You can tell a lot about a person based on the ways they engage with service industry personnel. In just a few hours of observing, I had made mental lists of the people who were good, solid to the core, and the people who likely thought the world owed them for something that had happened when they were young. As if an early check-in today would make up for all the misfortunes in their lives.

It was a dynamic I had experienced firsthand plenty of times at the fudge shop, but there was something different about watching it happen at the inn. The lobby was an overall calm environment, the gateway to where you sleep. It was welcoming and friendly. Warm and homey. Approaching the desk with any level of hostility somehow felt wrong, even if it was the same as the shop.

I guess entitled people took that energy everywhere.

Around 11 AM, things slowed again, and Tory acknowledged my existence, "Hey, let me show you how to make keys for the new arrivals."

She navigated through the booking system and showed me how to assign rooms based on who was already there, what type of room they booked, and what was set to be cleaned first, "All you have to do is click around, and voila. They are all set."

The interface of the software, like everything else on the island, looked historic with bold white letters on a black screen, but nevertheless, I nodded as if I fully understood the legacy reservation management system and would be able to replicate the ten-step process without fail. I would make it work though. If I could figure out this system, I could probably go to any hotel in the world and figure theirs out. How many places were working off software from the dawn of computers?

"We switched to digital key cards this season, but the system is still a little wonky. Can you help?" Tory showed me how to program the keys and pre-package them in little envelopes with the guest's name and room number. "All set? Why don't you call everyone on this list and let them know we could accommodate an early check-in whenever they find their way back to central Main Street?"

She tossed a clipboard in my direction.

"On it boss," I smiled, feeling like Tory and I were

bonding for the first time this summer when in reality she probably just enjoyed pawning off some of her tasks.

Luckily for both of us, I was her willing victim.

"Hello, this is Ella calling from the Inn. We are able to accommodate an early check-in for you. Please feel free to swing by whenever you're ready."

I worked my way down the list, checking names off one by one on the clipboard and prioritizing based on those who had been friendliest when they first arrived. Funny how voicing a desire for better service could backfire, I giggled under my breath, happy to have a little power to reward the nice guests. As my purple pen made its way to the last name on the list, the door flung open, with our new guests.

"Hi, dear. You said our room was ready?" A family of five filed into the lobby, filling the main area across our desk. I immediately recognized them as my first call. "I am so glad. We had an early morning wake-up call to get here so soon. It will be great to freshen up. We have a big day planned. First a ride around the island, then afternoon tea at the Grand Hotel! By the way, which fudge shop do you recommend?"

Most everyone came into the Inn so excited, sharing every last detail of their plans for the island. There was an element to the interaction that was deeper than I could achieve in a quick transaction at the fudge shop, and I was thriving.

Helping one family bring their bags to their room, I learned that they had three generations here with them, and each had been coming to the island since they were children. It was an annual tradition to come here, sample fudge from every shop to see who had the best that year, and bike around to the top destinations. For a week every year, for the past 30 years, this Inn had been their summer home. I was glad I had called them second.

In the afternoon, Tory suggested I go work in housekeeping. A few women took me around to the rooms. One had often worked with me in the fudge shop; she was from Jamaica and worked two jobs all summer to save up for winter back home with her family. She was amazing and showed me how to scrub a toilet, check a mattress for bed bugs, and change bedding—all in under five minutes. I made mental notes of each task, paying extra attention to the bed bug thing. There was no chance I would be checking into a hotel without dragging my finger along the seam of the mattress ever again.

After learning all the tricks to quickly clean the rooms and making sure that everything was somehow both spotless and cozy, the markings of a quality inn, it was time to go back to my actual job at the fudge shop.

My stomach dropped a little, knowing that it wouldn't bring me the same thrill. In just eight hours, I had fallen in love with working in the inn. Sure, you still had to deal with some grumpy guests, but the good ones were so much better. You got to know them. I also loved sitting in the cozy lobby, having paperwork to pass the slow moments by, and taking in the charm of it all.

Time passed by slowly as I spent the next eight hours on my feet. When I finally returned to the apartment later that night, there were passive-aggressive flyers pasted around every room. Memes telling people to take out their own trash and change the toilet paper roll when they finish one.

"Tory, did you see these signs? They're hilarious," I clamped my lips together, swallowing the sleepy laughs daring to escape my body, and reuniting with our room after my 16-hour workday.

"I put them there. People have been such a-holes, and I need to set them straight before they think they can act like slobs all summer. Did you even see the kitchen sink drain?"

"Oh, fair enough." I turned away to collect myself and, the people pleaser inside me, made a mental note to clean up after others to avoid this escalating into a real roomie conflict.

Living with six people was hard enough without the added stress of people fighting over literal trash.

The past few weeks there had been small moments of tension. Tory asked Andre if he'd lost his laundry basket when he left dirty socks in the middle of the living room. Tory called Veronica out for leaving her hair clumped on the side of the shower wall. Mike, who didn't even live here, somehow got a berating for leaving his beer cans on our windowsill. So far, I had managed to avoid Tory's line of fire, but all signs signaled one thing: if we didn't shape up, no one would be spared.

———

ANOTHER WEEK WENT by without me hearing about working at the Inn again. I knew disappointment. I had attempted to participate in online presale for the most recent sold-out tour. Even with two shows in Detroit, I was wait-listed. Not from my top choice university, but from buying concert tickets. This though felt far more personal.

I couldn't tell if it was something I did or just not a priority. Did Tory not want the extra work of dealing with me? Did Inez really not remember that I was supposed to shadow for at least 50 hours? The fudge shop was getting busier by the day, so I opted to focus on the positive: Violet wouldn't have wanted me preoccupied elsewhere, and I wouldn't have wanted to let her down.

TEN

Mackinac Island Travel Tip #10:
The Lilac Tree Festival is fully worth the hype.

IT WAS NEARING the end of June, and this week was going to be another busy one. It was the Lilac Tree Festival and our first sold-out weekend of the summer. The festival has been around for over 75 years and lasts ten days each summer. It is timed when the lilac trees, which populate the island, are in peak bloom and celebrates the lilacs' history on Mackinac. In an attempt to distract myself from the lack of hotel training I had gained so far this month, I threw myself into the festivities.

The festival includes a Lilac Queen coronation, a 10K, walking tours of the best and biggest trees, a parade, and live music in the park. The fudge makers had been grumbling all week about how they would need to work overtime every day, but I was buzzing with excitement for our first true busy week. I'd heard lore of the mid-summer crowds and was hoping to take on more responsibility to meet their demands.

"Emma, you ready for the crowds today?" I walked into the fudge shop, a huge smile plastered across my face.

"Bet. We just filled like ten garbage bags with folded boxes so when we don't have time to fold them today we can just grab them from the back. My hands are cramping, but I'm ready."

"Ella, can you sprinkle some of that pixie dust you've been drinking over here?" One of the fudge makers lamented from beyond the white picket fence that separated the fudge-making from the customers.

He was currently making a double dark chocolate mint and was grumpily moving in fast forward. How he could be that grumpy while engulfed in the sweet scent of chocolate was beyond me.

"Sorry for being positive!" I stuck out my tongue, happy to play the role of a real-life Disney princess in this situation.

I had biked around the island before my shift today, and the lilac trees had been stunning. Even the island air was so strongly infused with lilacs that it smelled like the guest bathroom in my grandmother's house. I fully understood why people came out of their way to be here this week and, if the town hadn't been already, I would have wanted to throw an entirc festival in the trees' honor. If that meant I was looking through life with lilac-colored glasses, so be it.

For the rest of my shift, I happily danced around behind the fudge counter, boxing up endless orders and gushing about the beautiful trees with our customers.

"Incoming. Unbutton the top of your polo," Emma whispered while moving quickly behind the counter.

"What?" I looked up quizzically.

"You'll thank me later!" She reached out and undid the button of my stiff olive green polo shirt, a uniform that flattered no one.

"Ella! Wow, it's crazy in here," George pushed his way

through the crowd and passed two other fudge clerks to a clearing opposite me at the counter.

Suddenly Emma's obsession with my buttons made sense. Too bad the shirt would always be unflattering, even if it were tailored to my exact dimensions instead of its current boxy polyester shape.

"Hey, George. What brings you in?" I tried to play it cool as if I hadn't been counting the moments since our last interaction.

"Oh you know, just heard this was the best fudge on the island."

"Oh, yeah? Where'd you hear that?"

"I work with this raving sugar addict, maybe you've met him? Chase?" he grinned, "he's claiming he can't get through the next two hours of his shift without a slice of fudge. Can you hook him up with your best flavor?"

"Is it actually for him, or is this one of those 'seeking advice for a friend' situations?" I mocked.

"Okay, fine. It's for both of us. Please?" He looked across the old-fashioned wooden counter with wide eyes, the burgundy on his Donnie's t-shirt popping against their swirling brown, green, and gold hues.

I would've given him the fudge either way, but giving him a hard time was worth it just to be looked at this way. My heart was melting faster than the fudge sitting in tourists' backpacks all around the sun-soaked island right now.

"Deal. You're getting my favorite of the day, Cookies and Cream."

I handed over the slice without a box and watched him disappear through the back room of the shop. The Donnie's guys didn't usually go that way, but there was such a crowd forming at the door and it was a smoother escape route.

———

"ARIELLA, can I bring you to your happy place for the night?" Emma busted through the front door of my apartment two hours later, already changed out of her polo and khakis and into a cute summer dress. "There is some insanity happening over at the park that I think you will like just as much as your precious lilac trees."

"Yes! I'll change quickly."

The park stood at the edge of the main strip of town, sprawling open green grass across from the harbor. There was a small statue in the middle, lilac trees framing the perimeter, and the historical forts of Mackinac perched high above, keeping a wary eye on the activity below. By the time we arrived, live music was in full swing with snack carts set up and people littering the grass with multicolored picnic blankets. We walked around, reading the menus and tracking which carts would beckon us back later on in the evening.

"Good evening everyone!" someone came on the mic, which sounded like it was surround sound despite there only being a few small speakers set up near the stone platform in the middle of the park. "We will be crowning our Lilac Queen soon, but before that, please join me at the edge of the lawn as we welcome back the winners of today's Lilac 10K!"

Shocked to see familiar faces beaded in sweat, I snapped some pictures, capturing George and his roommate Jack in high res as they crossed the finish line.

"STOP! Did you guys seriously do this?" We jogged over to the first and second-place race winners, crisscrossing our way through the crowd of tourists that had gathered at the lilac-colored finish line.

The crowd was tight, all pushing to the front in hopes their runners would be finishing next. Phones out, cameras open, flashes going off in all directions.

"How could we not? The grand prize is a $200 gift card to the Seahorse," Jack high-fived George, glowing at their victory.

"Hey, Ella," George smiled, "I didn't know you were coming to this."

"A festival in the park and the crowning of a new queen? I wouldn't miss it. I'm just glad we got here early enough to witness your big win."

Hyperaware of my facial experiences, I willed my muscles to keep my smile casual. We were clearly friends, but nothing more had happened, so I was toeing the water carefully with my pathetic attempts to flirt.

"OH! I love this song!" Emma gushed, grabbing my arm as Kid Rock started playing. These past few weeks she had grown quite fond of any song that mentioned Michigan. "Can we go sit? My legs are still exhausted from work."

"Imagine if you just ran a 10K," Jack gave her a dismissive look.

"You chose to do that. I didn't choose to stand for eight hours serving fudge. I mean, I guess I did, but either way. I'm sitting," she dragged me over to the pink towel we had discarded on the grass upon our arrival.

"Looks like you guys only have room for two, and we are pretty vile from our run. Want to meet back up in an hour for the Seahorse? I'll share my half of the winnings," George asked, Jack not following suit.

"Sounds like a plan," my eyes widened with anticipation.

The impromptu sharing of a prize counted as a date, right?

As they walked back toward the Purple House, Emma and I wandered around the various festival booths in the park, stopping only to make floral crowns out of lilacs. The hairpieces, tied around our heads with a ribbon bow, were deeply perfumed with a familiar blend, it was almost like roses mixed with warm vanilla sugar scrub. It was fragrant, yet fresh and I couldn't deduce how much was coming directly from the freshly cut lilacs and what was artificially added. Either way, I let the scent envelop me like a warm hug.

An hour later, after we watched Inez's 14-year-old daughter be crowned Lilac Queen (with a proper crystal tiara, not a lilac crown), we went to meet the boys at the Seahorse.

"Hello again!" We grabbed our spots at the table they had snagged on the back porch. "I can't believe you were able to get a seat outside tonight."

"Everyone is still over at the park. Plus, I know a guy," Jack winked at Emma, shooting his shot.

"We all know a guy. He comes in for free samples of fudge before every shift," Emma giggled, waving to the guy at the host stand.

Poor Jack, he didn't realize that Emma was already falling for Chase and any advances he tried to make were going to be in vain.

"So what are you guys up to for the rest of the night?" George turned his full attention to me.

"Probably just heading back to the Purple House after this. Tory's boyfriend's in town again, so I am going to have a slumber party with Emma and Sophie."

Sophie worked in the clothing store and was Emma's roommate. She was a nice girl who was plenty interesting to hang out with, but she opted to spend most of her time with the other boutique girls.

"Nice, us too."

We ordered a couple of appetizers, and the boys ordered two beers. Thinking they were being nice, the bartender sent over extras for me and Emma, knowing we worked next door, but not knowing that we hated beer. Or likely that we were both still underage.

"Chug on three?" Emma held her glass to the middle of the table.

"Chug on three," I hadn't chugged a beer before and the

bubbles tickled my throat, urging me to spit it back up with each passing gulp.

I willed myself to hold it down, counting down the seconds in my head, and somehow finished in only a few swigs more than Emma.

Other than the beer taste that lingered on my tongue, it was a fun and unexpected dinner. The only real problem? I still couldn't deduce if we were a group of platonic friends or a group of partially platonic friends with two friends who had a budding romance. Budding for him. Fully in bloom for me. If I had that fully bloomed flower in my hand right now and peeled off each petal, one by one, would it land on *he loves me* or *he loves me not*?

I pondered this question for longer than I would ever admit out loud as we headed back to the Purple House, still unsure of my metaphorical flower's fortune, I didn't know what to expect from the rest of the night. Was another evening of pretending to talk to people while keeping a side eye on George worthwhile, or should I just sneak off to Emma's room and go to bed?

When had I last felt this hopelessly obsessed with someone? I racked my brain for the only other time it had short-circuited this same way.

A single face floated into my mind and made itself at home there for the rest of the night: my junior-year lab partner.

ELEVEN

Mackinac Island Travel Tip #11:
Don't be afraid to explore beyond the main town: Some
of the best views are in the neighborhoods beyond the
bluffs.

IN MAJOR NEED of something salty after a long day in the fudge shop, I popped over to Donnie's around 4 PM. I was hopeful it would be slow, so they wouldn't mind giving me a doggie bag of all the leftover fries to enjoy on the break dock.

I had been driving myself crazy replaying each moment of the other night again, and again, a loop of self-inflicted torture. I was pretty sure George would be working and that I could once again try to ascertain if his lack of follow-through was because Emma was there or if he was just that uninterested in me. At the rate things were going, I had a sinking feeling that I would be ruminating on this all summer.

"Ella! I am dying. It has been so slow for the last half hour. How can no one want anything fried and greasy?" George handed me an extra large pop cup before I could even ask.

"Can I get you anything, gorgeous?" Andre came from the back and smiled at me with his extra wide, toothy grin.

"I got it, Andre. Take your break."

When the back door squeaked shut behind Andre, we were alone. I don't think I have ever been fully alone in Donnie's or even seen it with fewer than two tables of people. It must be a lull since it's the Monday before the weekend of the Fourth and the Lilac Tree Festival had recently ended. A calm between two storms.

"Do you have any leftover fries I can snag? I broke my own rules today and had one too many pieces of the sample fudge, and now I need to chase it down with something salty," I usually tried to limit myself to only one chocolate turtle or truffle per day and avoid the fudge entirely, which wasn't hard to do after staring at it all day, but today I had felt off.

Devouring my insecurities one sample-sized fudge bite at a time.

"I'll do you one better and make you some fresh fries and mozzarella sticks. The stuff in the back is starting to look a bit dodgy."

By fresh, he meant he would take them straight from the freezer, put them in the fryer, and then into a bag for me. Nevertheless, my heart fluttered at his inconsequential gesture. He was putting in extra work just for me. That had to mean something, right?

"Any chance you want to come..." His voice trailed off mid-sentence, turning his back slightly toward me as if to end the conversation.

Always flirty, but never forward.

"Come where?" I was growing more impatient by the day, a third of the summer was now ancient history, and I was not going to let him off this easily.

Even if he couldn't be forward, I could give it a try for once. I was done waiting. I had to try something.

"Uh, just around to the side to wait?" he pointed to an area off to the side as if I was in the way of some non-existent rush of people who would be joining us at any moment.

"Sure," I fought the urge to roll my eyes and stood off to the side.

I was being shoved to the side of the cash register in an entirely empty fast-food restaurant. This was a new low, even for me.

A few minutes later George handed me my 'fresh' and salty snacks. I could barely muffle a thank you under my breath, before moving toward the back exit and straight out to our little break dock. This is what my life had come to—looking forward to staring into the glistening abyss of a lake while eating my weight in fried cheese and potatoes. Which would actually sound pretty great if my love life had been anything other than nonexistent for the last 18 years, and I hadn't gotten my hopes up about that changing this summer. It was really my fault for ever expecting anything other than the status quo. What I really needed to learn this summer was how to stop playing with my own emotions and set my expectations.

"Ella, wait. What are you doing at six?"

"Hanging out with you?" I spun around on the heels of my sneakers and smiled shyly at George in hopes that hanging out was precisely what he was after.

If I was misreading the situation then I had misread this entire month and was willing to take the L.

"You read my mind," his toothy grin calmed my wavering confidence. "Meet me outside the Purple House later? Bring your bike."

I usually biked alone, mostly because if it wasn't between the hours of 11 PM and 7 AM, it was unlikely to have time off from work that lined up with someone who wanted to bike together, but I was beyond excited to explore with George.

The truth is, I would be excited to do just about anything with George.

I went out back to wipe down my bike, the purple metal slowly reemerging as I cleaned the splattered mud and horse unmentionables off its exterior. They really should have a bike wash on this island. I giggled, committing to tell Inez about the idea before the end of the summer.

———

I AUTOMATICALLY STARTED to take off on the Main road heading away from town when George suggested we go uphill into the island. I didn't normally go that way and was worried I might not be able to make it up the hill without having to walk my bike, but I agreeably went with what he wanted, lowering my gears to one and pushing through the harsh resistance with each pedal.

We climbed uphill passing the Grand Hotel and then turned left into the bluffs, and I pressed my palm to my forehead, absolutely speechless. I had heard this was the most insane neighborhood filled with beautiful private houses but had yet to experience them for myself, and they were even more spectacular than anyone had given them credit for.

Windy gravel roads wove through pastel mansions. Horses roamed small fenced-in yards, living their best lives atop the majestic island. Garage doors revealed small carriages for two. Lawns were decorated with brightly colored sculptures of flamingos and turtles. These were far and away the fanciest houses I had seen since being here, and I couldn't believe I hadn't ventured this way in the last few weeks.

We biked around for hours, passing the airport, which exclusively hosts private and charter planes, and ended up at the golf course. We biked through the course, all the golfers long gone for the day, and laughed about nothing as the sun set over the lake in the distance. Something about the post-9 PM northern Michigan sunset made it feel like we were truly alone on the island, on top of the hill far separated from all the people.

"I will never get used to how late it stays light here," George said, taking in the sky painted overhead in light water-color brush strokes of pink, orange, and pops of purple.

"Perks of being the furthest west in the Eastern Time Zone!" I smiled at the sunset, remembering the joy early summer brought to us as kids.

The days would grow longer and longer as spring turned to summer, and bedtime would get pushed later and later until the dusk of the night would have barely even set in at ten o'clock in the evening. It provided a magical veil of an endless day, prolonging the adventures and time spent outside.

"Have you been to The Woods?" George veered off the path and toward a row of golf carts which were neatly parked away for the night.

They were the first cars I had seen in weeks, and they weren't even cars.

"No... Is this not the woods?"

"No, the restaurant. It's owned by The Grand and has the best bar on the island," he pointed to an adorable green and red cabin down the road.

When had he been here before?

"Oh, I'm not twenty-one..." I dropped my chin to my chest, not wanting to remind him of my lack of experience.

"That's okay. It's a restaurant, so we can totally still go. Let's get a snack," eager for the night to continue, I followed him over to the bike lot where we ditched both our bikes before he led us into the quaint cabin.

He was right.

Despite its log cabin exterior, the bar was incredible. I knew it was summer, just a week before the Fourth, but I felt like I was at one of the ski lodges I would visit with my family growing up. Big leather couches and chairs. A working fireplace that left a smoky scent in the air. Plaid upholstery. It had everything you could expect of a cozy, upscale lodge. My stomach grumbled low, as if requesting a hot chocolate based on the environment alone.

"Don't let yourself be won over by the free popcorn, the actual best part of this place is the bowling," George ordered us two diet cokes, opting not to drink since I couldn't, and I tried to imagine any of the boys from high school making this, albeit small, sacrifice for me.

I knew for a fact—they simply wouldn't have.

I had offered to be the designated driver for my group at our junior year homecoming. After spending three hours getting ready with Mara, applying eyeshadow to match our dresses, and perfecting our beachy waves on a Michigan fall day, my date's older brother dropped him off at my house already tipsy. I propped him up for photos, shrugging it off when he stepped on my toes before I drove us to dinner. By the time we were halfway through the dance, he had downed another flask, so I took him home before he could get us both into trouble. Given I am still waiting for that thank you text, I can safely assume he would have never concerned himself with my comfort in a bar. That was the first and last time I bothered being set up for a school dance.

"Okay, I don't really know how to keep score, but are you up for a round?" I followed George through the bar and into a small back room where, sure enough, there were ten duckpins and mini bowling balls running the length of the building.

"No, but I'm sure we can figure it out," he walked over to the scoreboard, erasing the chalk left behind by the prior group.

"That will just make it easier for you to let me win," I

smiled, rolling the tiny ball down the lane in hopes it would knock over at least one of the pins.

Three of the ten pins fell to the floor with an aggressive thud.

"Oh no. I'll be putting up a fair fight," he rolled his own ball, missing all the pins, and then we both walked our way down the side of the lane to reset our pins. "Just kidding, I'll pretend I did that on purpose," he muttered under his breath.

"Thank you," I crinkled my nose, showing him I was in the on the joke, but would let him have it.

Things were going well. Honestly, I had never felt better at flirting. Our rapport came so naturally, that we lost track of time and spent the rest of the night eating as much popcorn as we could while getting endless free refills on our pops.

By the time he dropped me back at the big apartment, I was certain he was going to try to kiss me.

He didn't.

———

THE NEXT FEW days went by in a blur. George and I didn't make deliberate plans, but we met up every night after work. The group instinctively alternated between the Purple House and the big apartment, so we did too. We would fill our time with a mix of sneaking off for private conversations and joining in group drinking games. Neither of us wanted to fully retreat from the group and the other friendships we were forming, but also silently agreed that the time spent trading secrets on the front porch or the break dock was the highlight of any evening.

A small part of me wanted to push for something more to happen, but a larger part was so content with our friendship that I just let it continue to play out on his terms, as if afraid to spook the horse with a sudden movement.

One night, instead of our usual plans, Andre rallied a group of us to go night kayaking. One of his buddies was working at the kayak shack and had offered for us to go for free, after dusk. Walking up to the kayak booth, Emma, Andre, Chase, George, Mike, and Tory were all present and debating who would kayak with whom.

"Okay, but George and I have both never gone before. I am not about to get out there with him and let him flip us!" Emma exclaimed before throwing a subtle wink in my direction. "He should go with Ella, and I'll go with Mike." She grabbed Mike's arm and started off toward a teal-blue double kayak before he could voice an opinion.

"Guess you're with me," I clipped my own red life jacket over my pastel floral sweatshirt and capri leggings.

I had spent longer than usual trying to pick out an outfit for the evening. Finding something warm enough for the brisk evening that was also cute and could dry quickly if splashed was no small feat.

"It's my lucky night. What's your favorite color?" George grabbed two sets of paddles, turning toward the array of colorful kayaks and waiting to claim my favorite for us.

"Pink."

"This seems like the closest option," he nodded toward an orange kayak before securing his own life jacket. "Do you want the front or the back?"

"Definitely the front. Tallest goes in back," I hopped into the front without a second of hesitation, having kayaked plenty of times growing up. "Plus, this way you can mimic how I paddle."

"Great," he grunted, wobbling his way into the kayak and almost capsizing us before we were even a foot away from the shoreline. "Sorry, not the most graceful start."

"No worries. You good?" I hid the worry from my voice,

ALANA ROBIN

surprised at just how dark and desolate the world around us felt when floating on the lake at this time of night.

"I'm good. Ready to follow your lead, captain!"

"Great. It's easy. Left, right, left, right. Just keep an even tempo and go on each side. Try to stay in sync with me."

"What if we need to turn?" concern laced his voice, the usual confidence left on dry land.

"We aren't trying to go anywhere so we don't really need to turn," I laughed, taking in the stillness of the water and all of our friends who were still floating around within a few feet of us.

"You sure?"

"Positive, but if it makes you feel better. I will be in charge of steering."

"Okay, I'm trusting you, Ella. No taking me out to sea and leaving me to fend for myself," his accent made him sound slick and confident, but I was sure I'd heard a small quiver in the statement.

"Wouldn't dream of it," I pushed my paddle down into the water, gliding us forward, into the darkness, and I could feel George trying to mirror my motions from behind me. "How you doing back there?"

"I'm getting it. This is actually quite lovely," he smacked his paddle into mine and a splash ran through the air. He mumbled under his breath, "Bugger."

"Yeah, you're a natural," I giggled.

"Hey now, you don't know that I didn't do that on purpose," he splashed me again as we guided our kayak farther from the group.

"Okay, okay, what do I need to say for you to not splash me again with that icy cold water?" I turned around in my seat to face him.

"Tell me I am a quick learner," the confidence had fully returned to his voice and if the butterflies in my stomach didn't calm down soon, there was a good chance they were going to be the ones rocking the boat so hard that we ended up in the water.

He unclipped his life jacket before undoing the top button of his now wet jacket, and my eyes tracked each movement, watching as he undid one after another until he took the jacket off completely.

"You are a quick learner," I felt my cheeks flush and turned back toward the front of the kayak. "So quick in fact, why don't I just take a little break while you paddle?" I carefully placed my paddle across my lap, leaning back in the kayak and looking up. The boat was surrounded by a sparkle of fireflies, lighting the area around us in unison every few seconds, "I love fireflies."

"Wow," I heard George's paddle come to a rest as it squeaked against the plastic edge of the boat. We wobbled back and forth as he adjusted his position. I really hope he re-clipped that life jacket. "This is stunning."

"I think I could fall asleep out here."

Our bodies were being gently rocked by the small movements on the surface of the water. We both indulged in the silence for a while, neither one of us breaking the trance that had now encapsulated our little boat, keeping us separate from the chatter of our friends.

"These damn mosquitos are trying to give me some kind of disease."

All at once there was a smack and a splash. His paddle had gone overboard.

"You know you can be really dramatic sometimes?" I teased, pulling his paddle back into the boat. "Are you going to need me to take you in?"

"Yes, please. Save me from these creatures."

I probably should have been disappointed as we headed in, but I wasn't. This hadn't been our first date. It was a group hang, and I just got lucky (thank you, Emma!) to share a kayak with him. But it was also more than that. It was proof that I wasn't misreading everything and at the bare minimum: we were friends. Real friends. The kind who can sit in silence together and not have it feel awkward.

At least until the mosquitos attack.

TWELVE

Mackinac Island Travel Tip #12:
To avoid crowds, don't travel the week of the Fourth.
But if you must, find a beach with a view of the
Mackinac Bridge for the firework show.

IN ANY TOWN with a primary trade in tourism, the Fourth is a busy week. Eight-hour shifts become nine with the nightly clean-up and prep for the next day bleeding into the late evening hours.

I wound up scheduled on the closing shift on the third and the opening shift on the fourth—a combination that left you with very little sleep, but also a lot of free time. Two island half days in a row.

The morning of the third, I woke up around 9 AM and slowly started my day. I walked down Main Street thinking that I could grab a fancy latte at the other Rosanna's location (they had an espresso machine, and we didn't), but I quickly realized that I needed to get away from the crowds if I wanted to relax at all.

I decided to bike up into the bluffs. The area had instantly become one of my favorite places on the island since George had shown it to me last week. As I rode by each house, I imagined my life there. I named the horses and pictured my family, all gathered around on the porch enjoying the view. There was one house in particular that I loved. It was a light yellow with pink trim and had a little circular driveway that was just wide enough for a bike. The shutters had pink and white stripes, and they had pink turtle sculptures scattered throughout the garden. It was whimsical and looked like exactly the kind of garden you could spend an entire day in just reading and sunbathing.

The best part though was the personal stable. It was just off to the side with a little carriage sitting under an open garage with two white horses roaming in the lawn adjacent. A not-so-modern-day fairytale.

I couldn't believe how many houses were sitting empty. What was the point of owning a house like that if you weren't even using it on the Fourth of July?

If it were mine, I would promptly plop myself on that porch and take reading breaks feeding my horse friends. I was still thinking about that alternate universe when I arrived for my shift at three.

The closing shift was always crazy, but it was full-blown madness that afternoon. From the minute I got there, there wasn't a moment to spare for even a short break. We were continuously running out of boxes and the guys were working overtime to keep all the fudge flavors on the shelf.

At one point, I was even asked to carry two trays of chocolate peanut butter down the street to our other location because they had sold out and couldn't make a new batch fast enough. At the risk of being incredibly dramatic, trays of fudge are heavy. Dodging tourists is hard. Doing both on the

Fourth of July weekend? Nearly impossible. I'm shocked the fudge didn't end up in the middle of the street mixed in with the horse droppings and other unidentifiable substances. If it had, I just know I would have been lying on the ground in the middle of it all, trampled. A shiver rolled through my body just thinking about it.

When 11 rolled around, I was both overjoyed and exhausted.

"So sorry, we're closed. We will open again tomorrow morning," I yelled to the squeak of the screen door without even bothering to turn around.

"Hey, Ella. It's me. Brutal day, huh?" I recognized George's voice instantly.

"The. Worst. There was a family of ten that were all screaming ice cream flavors at me until the last minute. I might just pass out right here on this cold tile floor for the night."

"Well, if you decided not to, I was thinking of going over to Isle Manor and crashing their s'mores set up. Want to come?"

I did want to. More than anything.

"I have to open tomorrow, so I need to be back here at eight..." My voice trailed off as my internal monologue calculated what time I needed to be in bed to get at least six hours of sleep.

I also pondered if six hours could possibly be enough before the rush we would be welcoming on the fourth.

"Forget it. That is brutal, and it will probably be too crowded anyway. Are you going to go to the north beach tomorrow?" George questioned, holding still in anticipation of my response.

"I think so. Are you? If not, I could probably make tonight work for an hour or so..."

This was it. He was finally taking the initiative that I had been waiting for, and I'd be damned if stupid work was going to get in the way. I had my whole life to work, but who knew how many nights a cute boy from London would be inviting me to make s'mores. Right?

"No, let's do it tomorrow. I have the 10 AM shift tomorrow anyway and should get some sleep, too. I'll catch you in the evening, and maybe we can head over to the beach together around eight?" George asked.

"Definitely."

The screen door slammed, and I ambled over to lock it as quickly as my tired legs could take me. I couldn't risk anyone else coming in who was genuinely seeking fudge.

———

THE CROWD MAY HAVE BEEN DEMANDING, but my shift flew by faster than ever before. It was a stellar combination of hustling too hard to notice the time and nervous energy for the evening ahead.

Luckily, I had time for a quick nap and shower before George was planning to pick me up. I carefully put on my best jean shorts and an ironic American flag sweater that I had thrifted before the summer started. Mara had assured me it was cute without trying too hard as we did our makeup together over a video call. With her stamp of approval, I was ready.

"Hey! Are we biking or walking?" George had walked right into the living room without even bothering to knock.

The pros and cons of working and living with over 30 people, including your crush. At least this was better than when Mike walked in wasted last week, puked in the kitchen sink, and then left without even acknowledging my presence on the couch...

"Let's walk. It will be way easier with the crowds," George

effortlessly grabbed my hand, as if we had walked hand-in-hand together a million times before.

I made a silent wish that they would stay dry and that no clammy stickiness would betray me tonight. Maybe he did want to be more than friends...

The walk from Main Street to the north beach was not that long, but we strolled slowly stretching out our alone time —if you count walking down a street with thousands of tourists alone time—as long as possible. It was such a slow walk that I was almost surprised when we didn't loop back around the block before finally approaching the beach.

"You guys made it!" Emma waved us over to her, winking at our hands which were still interlocked.

She was so good at winking that a small pang of jealousy flowed through me. The beach was all stones, like many in northern Michigan, and everyone was sitting on towels that were folded two or three times to limit the pain of the rocks poking from the ground beneath.

Despite the discomfort, I loved the stone beaches of Mackinac. They reminded me of growing up when we would hunt for Petoskey stones on the beach instead of sea shells to take home to polish. My sister, Abigail, and I would always fight over who would get the one with the prettiest fossil patterns hidden under its lackluster surface. One year, we even set up a stand, akin to a lemonade stand, and tried to sell our best rocks to our neighbors during their evening strolls through the neighborhood. Whoever sold a stone to the highest bidder would win bragging rights for a week.

"Hey! Have you been here long?" I called back as George released my hand to greet the others.

"Not at all. Chase has been trying to start this fire the whole time though. No luck," Emma giggled while simultaneously rolling her eyes in his direction.

"It's harder than it looks, okay? We don't have any twigs

and honestly, I'm two minutes away from dumping out one of the Popov bottles and lighting it on fire."

"There might be hope yet," Emma was clearly unconcerned with wasting our $7 vodka.

"I'll help you, mate," George gathered pieces of beer boxes and built them up as fire starters.

Soon, there was a little box pyramid in the center of the circle of stones with three logs surrounding it. With 20 of us gathered around, our collective breath held tight as we watched George's project... the fire caught.

"Alright! Shots for everyone to celebrate!" Chase took a large swing from the Popov bottle that was still waiting on standby in his hand, thrilled that his duties for the night were done and that his drink of choice had been spared a fiery death.

Andre turned on some music, Jared grilled up some hot dogs, everyone's s'mores were roasting, and before long we were all singing Kid Rock at the top of our lungs because it was indeed Northern Michigan during the summertime.

"Ella, are you seriously just letting that marshmallow go up in flames?" George accused while slowly working to get the perfect golden brown to his own. "I'm shocked you're a burnt marshmallow fan. I always thought only impatient people did that."

Oh George, if only you knew just how impatient I really am.

"Yes, this is without a doubt the only right way to do it. I'll make you one next to prove it."

I took a big bite, melty marshmallow sticking across my chin. George slowly wiped it away with the pad of his thumb, momentarily forgetting his disapproval of my roasting preferences, our eyes locked. I was suddenly very aware of the sound of my own heartbeat. I wanted to reach out and touch George.

I wanted him to kiss me. Licking the last remnants of marshmallow from my lips, I dared him to.

He didn't. Instead, he turned back toward the lake, as if nothing happened.

The moon was reflecting off the lake, and the Mackinac Bridge was glistening in the distance. The sun had just set, and fireworks were about to start. My sweater was wrapped tightly around my body, providing only a thin layer of separation between us. The cool summer breeze mixed with the smell of burnt sugar. *Everything was still perfect. It could still happen tonight.*

We moved down the beach a little ways away from our friends and coworkers as the chorus of fireworks roared into the dark sky. Sharing a towel, we leaned back on the rocks, curved together in a crevice between two bigger boulders. Colors rocketed through the sky as each firework flashed in the distance, their pink, green, red, blue, and white reflections lighting up the wavy surface of the lake with each pop.

I had always loved fireworks but had never shared them with anyone special. Sitting here, leaning softly against George, fingers sticky with marshmallows, I could not imagine a more picture-perfect moment. This scene didn't even need me to romanticize it beyond reality. It was an idyllic summer night, a jar filled with lightning bugs, glowing from within.

———

"ELLA! How was the rest of your night? Did things finally leave the friend zone with George?" Emma was already behind the counter, dutifully folding fudge boxes.

"No. I don't get it. Things were going so well, that I even converted him to a burnt marshmallow lover, and then, nothing. He dropped me back here and immediately went back to the Purple House without a second look back," I was defeated, clearly reading all the signs wrong.

I'd had crushes in high school and had gone on a handful of dates, but this was proof I didn't know the first thing about guys. We were obviously just friends, and I was foolishly mistaking his ounce of attention as a sign of unwavering love.

I'd spent the night tossing and turning, trying to convince myself that I was here to work anyway. I was happy we were just friends. Friends weren't distracting. Friends cheered you on as you worked toward your goals. Friends could keep in touch beyond summer, and friends were great. I loved friends.

"That makes no sense. He didn't even look at anyone other than you last night. Maybe he's just nervous?" Emma had quickly become the best, most supportive summer friend I could have imagined.

One that I really did love. An older sister, looking after me and hyping me up when I needed it most. On busy days spent behind the fudge counter, her words of encouragement were welcomed and appreciated, but right now I was craving Mara's tougher love and a frank reality check.

"Maybe..."

"Can I try the chocolate peanut butter?" A fudgie abruptly interrupted us, and we got to work.

The Fifth of July rush was proving to be just as grueling as the days prior.

I worked straight through my lunch break and barely got a moment to step out from behind the counter for a sip of water. By the time I got off, all I wanted to do was flop on my bed. I heated a Buffalo chicken hot pocket and sat alone on the worn-out floral couch in the living room, slowly eating my less-than-gourmet meal in a trance.

"Ouch," my impatience burned the roof of my mouth.

This day was only getting worse, and I needed to get out of this funk. After a long hot shower, I video-called Mara.

"How was the rest of your Fourth?" I asked her.

She gave me all the details of her family's night at the lake, down to which was her favorite new side dish for a barbecue. Mexican street corn grilled on the cob. Just as she was taking my mind off things, the door to the apartment slammed. It must have been Chase or Andre, finished for the night.

"Ella, are you home?"

I sprung up from my bed to see George standing in the doorway of my bedroom, still in his Donnie's uniform.

"Mara, I'll call you back," I hung up the phone, shocked to see him after how things ended last night, but I tried to play it cool, hoping he wouldn't comment on my cheetah print pajamas or the mess of Tory's clothing sprawled across the floor. "Hey, what's up?"

"Oh you know, just spent the day saving the masses from their hangovers one greasy burger at a time." *His accent was so cute. Why, oh why, did he not feel the same way? Midwest accents could be charming too, right?* "So, I had a really great time with you last night."

"You did?" My mouth gaped open, revealing my inner thoughts, while the corners of George's mouth turned halfway up, apprehensively unable to commit to a full smile.

"Of course I did. Wasn't it obvious?"

"Well, I thought so. But then I wasn't sure..."

"Well, I did. And I want to hang out again, just us." He looked almost as nervous as the hot pocket in my stomach had started to feel—wavering on the edge of eruption.

"Yeah?" I had heard that before with the bike ride and the walk to the Fourth.

Was this time going to be different?

"Yeah. You want to also, right?" His voice cracked, and I realized for the first time that these feelings might be new for him too.

He could also be scared. He could be wondering if this was

all in his head. I might not be the only one spiraling down the self-doubt rollercoaster.

"Yeah, I would like that," I reassured him with a soft smile.

Even though we still had no set plans, my mood was fixed. That night, I drifted off to sleep with that smile still extending across my face.

THIRTEEN

Mackinac Island Travel Tip #13:
Be kind to your servers, you'll see them out later.

WALKING through the double doors of Hotel Waldenwood, the open air, and tall ceilings immediately greeted me with a sweeping view of the lake. Colorful chairs were lining the lobby with suitcases tucked in each corner, all marked with fluorescent tags in pink, green, and yellow. The air reeked of eucalyptus as if it was piped through the vents to mask the mixture of fudge and horse poop that veiled the rest of the island.

People mulled about, yelling across the lobby for their kids to stop running and juggling shopping bags from all the stores on Main Street.

I wasn't clear on why Inez had asked for me to come by today, but I was hoping she had remembered my work credits and that my shadowing would begin more formally for my final month and a half on the island. The summer was officially halfway over, and I had still only worked one day at the

Inn. As I made my way through the bustling hotel lobby, I crossed my fingers that there was more for me to do over here.

"Ella, thank you so much for coming over on such short notice. This is Dorothea." She waved to a stunning blonde woman who appeared to be in her thirties. She had kind eyes with slight wrinkles that I guessed were from spending her days smiling so widely. "Dorothea manages the front office here at the Hotel Waldenwood. Come join us."

Inez patted softly on the blue and white striped couch, her posture calm and collected.

"I'm sure you're wondering why you're here. I know your shadowing hasn't been as consistent as you may have hoped, but I think we found a solution for that. One of Dorothea's front desk agents had to leave the island unexpectedly, and we are in a bit of a pickle. Getting someone new to come to the island mid-season is not easy, so I was wondering how you would feel about taking on some new work."

"Wow, thank you. I'm so honored you thought of me, but how would that work with my current job? I can't leave Violet short-staffed," I definitely could and would if Inez said to.

"You would continue your role at the fudge shop five days a week instead of six and then you could work here five days a week as well. Dorothea and Violet would coordinate your schedule to stagger your morning and evening shifts and you would have at least one full day off a week, the same as you currently do. You'd also have two days a week where you only work one of the jobs.

"The four days a week that you work both jobs would be long, sixteen hours, but the pay over here would be $4 more per hour. You can save up a bit more before school! Plus the experience would be invaluable."

She was trying to sell me on it without realizing this needed no sales pitch. The hours would be long, but, if my mental math was right, this would give me two hundred hours of work credit before college even started. That was four times my goal for the summer. Also, 4 dollars extra an hour? That was one and a half times my rate at the fudge shop. I had never made that much before, having been rejected by plenty of jobs less desirable than this, but I guess it's true what they say. Life is all about being in the right place at the right time.

"I'd love to. When can I start?" I beamed as if having won a prize and not having just committed to an unfathomable workload.

"Oh, I'm thrilled! We need to work out your schedule for the next week, but why don't you start tomorrow? You'll be here from 7 AM to 3 PM and at the fudge shop from 3 PM to 11 PM. Sounds good?"

"Yeah, that's great. What should I wear here?"

I pulled at the hem of my shirt, the overwhelm of my new schedule starting to sink in. Before this summer, I barely stayed awake from 7 AM to 11 PM, let alone worked for that long. My brows furrowed as I realized that the hotel was even classier than the Inn and, despite being the exact same clientele as the fudge shop, would require a more elevated level of service than I knew how to provide. I pushed the fears aside, reassuring myself that I had always been a quick study. This didn't need to be any different.

"That's the thing. There's no set uniform over here for the front desk. It's nice dresses, blazers, blouses and skirts, no sandals or sneakers. Do you have any of that with you?" Dorothea raised her perfectly maintained brows at my current attire, which was a Rosanna's olive green polo and khaki capri pants.

"Totally. I'll be great," I tried to mask the shaky panic in my voice, replacing it with my earlier joy.

I had two sundresses and the one outfit I had brought for the Inn, but definitely nothing as nice as what Dorothea was wearing, and the only clothing shop on the island was geared toward tourists which meant I could not afford it. Even if I could, I would be hard-pressed to find an entire wardrobe that was work-appropriate in their summer collection of flowy sundresses and brightly-colored beach attire.

After quick goodbyes, I frantically dialed my mom to have her overnight me the business casual clothes from my days in the Future Business Professionals of America club at my high school. I caught her up on the rollercoaster of a conversation, still trying to process my feelings about the situation, as she walked through the closet with me on the line. She would send my black ballet flats, a few black skirts, some colorful blouses that I could dress up, and a gray linen blazer that I could wear with everything.

With my attire settled, I scrolled through the history of the Hotel Waldenwood on their website, forcing each key point to memory as if there would be a quiz in my near future. The hotel had been around for over one hundred years and had won numerous awards for excellence in service. It featured a restaurant with live music on Wednesdays and Saturdays, and they appeared to already be fully booked for most nights in July and August with an average daily rate of $450. Armed with the promise of a new wardrobe arriving in three to five business days and all the knowledge Google could provide, I managed my way through my afternoon shift at the shop.

———

THE NEXT MORNING, I arrived at the Hotel Waldenwood at 6:45 AM in my best sundress, only cardigan, and dressiest sandals—ready to go. I walked directly to the front desk, unsure where else to go and realizing they had set absolutely zero expectations yesterday.

Dorothea gave my outfit a quick glance, but to her credit did not comment on how terrible it was. We walked a full tour of the property, starting first in the back of house. It housed the largest laundry room I had ever seen with two walls flanked by over a dozen washing machines, dryers, and shelves upon shelves of cleaning products neatly tucked into color-coordinated rows. The tour continued through the industrial kitchen, a storage space filled with extra pillows and blankets, and there was even a small hidden storage room teeming with colorful shirts and souvenirs sold at a boutique in the lobby. After we wound through the maze of the back of house, we walked through the restaurant, an assortment of guest rooms (queen, king, double queen, suites), and across the pool deck before ending at my new home—the front desk.

"Thank you for jumping in so quickly to help us. I know it will be a lot of work for you, but we really appreciate it. I'll make sure to teach you everything I know."

Her posture was perfect, but her overall energy was somehow still warm and inviting. Standing up a little straighter myself, I idolized her already.

"First things first, this is the desk. You will spend most of your time here." She pulled the largest binder I have ever seen out from under a stack of clipboards. "This right here, it has everything you need to know. Extensions for all the other hotels on the island, secret numbers for last-minute reservations, numbers for cleaning or dock porters, and a guide to all the codes you will find on the computer. Any slow minute the next few days, you read this."

I flipped my finger through the pink and green tabs of the book, stopping on a page with recommendations for different guests segmented by their characteristics. What to recommend if it's a family with young kids, which of those not to recommend if they have a grandparent with them, and so on. It was meticulously organized, and I absolutely loved it.

"This is the phone. Don't let it intimidate you," she gestured to the phone, talking me through the thirty-plus buttons and how to place someone on hold before walking me through the computer.

The reservation management system, though similar to the one at Tory's Inn, looked complicated, but I told Dorothea I was confident that after a few days, I would get the hang of it.

When I arrived here yesterday, I noticed the decor. The playful seahorse lampstands. The expansive view of the lake that was framed by the dining room of the hotel restaurant. The colorful patterns in the rug looked like they belonged in a magazine. Those thoughtful details, still prominent in the room, were no longer my focus. I had been let in on the secret to what made this place look so effortlessly beautiful.

The guests saw a swanky room where they were greeted by the lake breeze. I saw a room filled with the potential of my chosen career path. A place where I could make dreams come true by simply dialing a secret phone number or suggesting the perfect restaurant that someone would reference as their best vacation memory for decades to come. It was the first moment that summer when I felt truly confident in the decisions I had made that led me here. That would lead me to a lifelong career in this industry.

Three hours of training later, Dorothea trusted me to answer the phones.

"Good morning, thank you for calling the Hotel Waldenwood. This is Ariella speaking. How can I assist you today?" I read off a script that was printed on a torn sheet of paper, dangling from the back of the desk by a worn piece of scotch tape.

"You'd like a double queen room? End of August?" I struggled to work my way through the computer while juggling the phone. "It does look like we have availability. Would you like to give me a credit card now? Great."

I completed the booking and felt so proud. I was doing this.

"A few tips..." Dorothea didn't wait long to burst my bubble. "It's much easier to work the reservation system if you don't play with your hair while you're on the phone. It'll free up both hands. Also, always say 'of course' when a guest asks for something. Never question back or just say 'good.'"

For the rest of the shift Dorothea stayed at my side, coughing quietly anytime I said 'yes' or 'sounds good' and poking my side when I twirled my hair between my fingers. It would have been incredibly obnoxious if I weren't so grateful for the training. Grateful and a bit embarrassed.

"Hey, Ella! When did you start working here?" Jared came barreling through the front door with five suitcases and two fudgies in tow.

"About four hours ago," I laughed awkwardly.

"That's awesome. You done at Rosanna's?"

"Nope, doing both. It'll be good for me to save money for school."

I figured saving money was more relatable than being a total dork who really wanted to learn about hotels firsthand, and it wasn't a lie. Just not my primary motivator at the moment. Something told me Jared would not quite understand that I was enjoying Dorothea's watchful eye and eager to present myself more professionally.

"That's great. Well, check-in isn't for a few hours so can you give me some tags for this luggage and then take their info down?" Jared gracefully tossed all the luggage in the corner as if they weighed nothing.

"Of course," I said proudly, glancing to the side to see if Dorothea noticed, but naturally it was the one moment she had left me alone all morning.

I passed him five fluorescent tags that he quickly scribbled on from the other side of the front desk.

"Cool. I gotta get back to the docks, but I'll be seeing you very soon," he smirked before sprinting back out to his bike.

And he was right. He was back every ten minutes for the remainder of the shift, repeatedly barging through the door with a stack of baggage.

———

I'M NOT sure who Jared usually spent his time with. He was a local, and everyone working on the island knew the locals. It was like being a celebrity on an island of thousands of people during the summer months—except you spent the other half of the year living with only a few hundred other people on the island. An island of only those summer celebrities. I'd only seen Jared socially at the Fourth, but we were becoming fast friends now that we worked together, so I wasn't that surprised to see him show up at the Purple House a couple of nights after my first day at the hotel.

"Ella! What are you having? I brought you something better," Jared sauntered in with a level of confidence that only someone who grew up on the island could have when entering a house they didn't live in.

Over the years, he had lived in pretty much all of Inez's employee housing, including my apartment and this house.

"Honestly, that wouldn't be hard to do. It's Bud Light," I frowned at the nearly full beer in my hand.

As much as I had gotten used to being around people drinking this summer, I still tried to limit myself to one drink most nights, and even that I barely ever finished. On the island, you can get a DUI for biking while drunk, and there was no chance in hell I was going to tempt fate into ruining my entire future for a cheap drink in a house of people I would have to see at work the next day.

"Have this instead. You might actually get through more

than a few sips," he handed me an extra large spiked seltzer can in the flavor watermelon.

Was he flirting? It felt like flirting, but he was so much older and was maybe just being nice. I'm sure that was it. Besides, I was with George now. Or was I? I honestly wasn't even sure.

"So what's the college crew doing for fun these days, anyway?" Jared snuck a disapproving glance around the room, popping his own can open and tilting it in my direction.

Our cans met with a clink and we each took a sip, mine small and his gulping up half the can.

"You're looking at it," I waved my arms around to everyone chatting, playing cards, and listening to music.

It was a very typical night for us.

"Oh, well, surely we can do better than this," Jared failed to mask the disappointment on his face, although I am not sure he even tried to hide it. "My buddy is the bouncer over at The Bridge Bar. You want to go?"

"Are you sure that's okay? Emma and I aren't twenty-one yet," I peered apprehensively at Emma who also needed help getting in, and then at George who was already 21 and often skipped the bar scene to hang with us.

"Bet. Let's do it."

We hightailed it back to Main Street, struggling to keep up with Jared's large strides, and as promised, we had no trouble getting into the Bridge. Everywhere I looked in the bar was a different shade of wood, a mixture of various faux leather and mahogany chairs dotting each table. The air was filled with a sweet summer breeze from the open windows and the live music blanketed the space. There were cheers and laughter as people played darts and competed on a vintage Pacman machine at the edges of the room. The culmination of everything was a scene I hadn't experienced elsewhere on the island

—the magic of locals, summer workers and guests seamlessly mixing as one.

Skipping the bar, I focused on the Pac-Man machine. After spending many Saturdays of my youth at the vintage arcade in downtown Ann Arbor, I was practically an expert, but no one here knew that.

"Sorry, I win," I mocked George, raising my eyebrows with faux pity.

"Pretty sure you just hustled me," George chuckled, "I want a rematch."

He clicked a few buttons on the glowing blue screen and rebooted the game.

My feet still ached from working two jobs, and I was running on very little sleep, but I was content. This was the Mackinac Island experience I had read about online, and this moment, and a string of many moments like this, was what summer was all about. The summer wouldn't be measured by the time spent working, but instead by these bits of time in between.

Working at the Hotel Waldenwood was proving to have some unexpected perks.

FOURTEEN

**Mackinac Island Travel Tip #14:
You never know who you might run into.**

THE FOLLOWING MORNING, I was not feeling my best as I shuffled into the hotel for the opening shift, but I gradually pulled it together. I ambled around behind the front desk going through the motions, checking people in, answering phones, and acting like I knew exactly what I was doing; meanwhile, I was so out of it, that when Jared brought in a family and their bags around 11 AM, I almost didn't recognize them.

"Ariella Abrams! What are you doing here?" Standing before me was Eric Zhang, my unrequited high school crush, sandwiched between his parents and looking far more excited to see me than he had ever demonstrated in the decade I had known him.

"I'm working here for the summer, and also over at Rosanna's, the best fudge shop on the island! Can I help get you all settled for your stay?" Palms sweating, I quickly typed his last name into the reservation system to see how long they'd be there.

Three nights.

"That would be great. It's under Zhang," his dad approached the desk, woefully unaware that I had spent the last four years idolizing his son.

Eric was the star of the school hockey team, and he was headed to MIT this fall. He was a rare blend of brainy and sporty that usually only existed in movies. He also had the friendliest smile to ever grace the face of a jock.

"Of course, sir. I see we have you staying with us for three nights in a two-bedroom suite overlooking the lake. Unfortunately, it is a bit before check-in, but I can take down your number and call as soon as the room is ready. Would that work well for you?" I handed Mr. Zhang the clipboard over the desk, doing my best to regurgitate the check-in script that Dorothea had taught me just a few days prior.

"Ella has my number already, Dad. We were in the same group for our science project junior year," Eric pushed the clipboard back over the wooden desk, and my head automatically tilted to the side.

It was only a month-long project, and while it solidified my obsession with him, I was certain he had barely realized I was there, or that I had saved his number. I guess I had underestimated myself...

"Great. We will just wait for you to call Eric. Any recommendations on what to do in the meantime?" Mr. Zhang asked.

I quickly recommended the best place to rent bikes, or at least the one the magical book told me was the best, and a ride around the island. I told them it would take about an hour, and gave them Rosanna's Fudge coupons for when they returned.

As they walked out of the Hotel Waldenwood, I smiled proudly. I had not only crushed playing it cool but also remembered everything from my training. Even on just a handful of hours of sleep.

The rest of my shift at the hotel went by quickly, a blur of exchanging plastic room keys for fluorescent bag tags, and then starting over in the reverse. Eight hours and two bitter coffees later, I wrapped up my day at the fudge shop.

"Ella. You are everywhere, aren't you?" Mr. Zhang walked in, his helmet knocking against the glass of the fudge counter as it dangled carelessly from his wrist.

"Just trying to put in the work before school starts in a couple of months," I cloaked the pounding exhaustion with my signature ever-present smile, straightening up behind the counter and gently smoothing out my polo shirt.

"Dad, Ella is going to Cornell to study hospitality. Isn't that cool?"

Eric knew what I was going to be majoring in? I felt my cheeks flush as I busied my hands shuffling supplies behind the fudge counter. Maybe I really had made as much of an impression on him as he had on me during our science project...

"Well, in that case, this seems like the best place for you to be spending your summer. I kept trying to get Eric to do something worthwhile this summer, but all he wants to do is teach hockey camp at the rink," Mr. Zhang rolled his eyes, and I tried not to flinch as his helmet clinked against the glass display case for the tenth time.

"It's the last time I get to play," Eric grumbled under his breath, indicating that they had this conversation before, and he didn't want to rehash everything in front of me.

"Can I get you some samples?" I changed the subject and passed them larger-than-typical samples of all my favorites. "The dark chocolate sea salt caramel will change your life."

I watched their expressions change with each bite and carefully wrapped up two three-packs, but, leveraging my only power in this shop, I only charged them for five slices.

When my shift finally ended, I clocked out and dragged my sleepy body up to the apartment. No one was home, so I flopped onto the couch and pulled out my phone to call Mara. She wasn't going to believe that Eric was here.

One unread text flashed across my lock screen.

ERIC ZHANG

Where'd you go? I was waiting outside the shop for you to get off, but you never came out.

He was waiting for me? Should I go meet him? What about George? Was there even a George? What would I possibly reply?

ERIC ZHANG

Do you want to hang out for a bit?

A double text. My hand quivered as I contemplated the appropriate response, typing, deleting, and retyping the same message.

ELLA

I live upstairs so I came the back way. Let me meet you out front.

I don't know why I am still wearing a full face of makeup to work in a fudge shop, but at least it makes this changing routine easier. I flung my body around the room, quickly changing out of my polo and khakis and into a casual navy t-shirt dress before taking the stairs two at a time and walking around the side of the building.

There he was. Eric Zhang. Standing on Main Street. Waiting for me outside Rosanna's.

"Hey, sorry. How long have you been here?"

"Well, you mentioned you were closing and the shop

closed at 11, so I've been here since about 10:45. I didn't want to miss you." He had been waiting for over half an hour. "In hindsight, I probably should have just come in and told you I'd be waiting outside, but this seemed romantic."

"That's so sweet of you."

Was this really happening? And why did he care about making it romantic?

"Anyway, my parents called it a night, but I thought we could hang out?" He questioned, sheepishly.

"Yeah…" Was this a betrayal to George? We hadn't even kissed and certainly had not DTR (defined the relationship). Maybe we were just friends… "Yeah, that would be great. The only thing is, I have to work again at seven, so I can't really hang for too long."

"Totally. Any time that you have is worth it to me. What do you like to do around here?"

"We could grab some ice cream, and go for a walk down to the harbor?"

"Perfect!"

Attempting to show off, I brought Eric around back and into the fudge shop through the back office. We were careful to only turn on one light before tiptoeing over to the ice cream case.

"What's your favorite?" I asked, watching his eyes dart around the display case, taking in all 20 flavors of ice cream. It was made locally on the mainland and, though I would never tell anyone I thought this, was even better than our fudge.

"Surprise me," he said.

I scooped us both two large waffle cones of my personal favorite flavor, Mackinac Island Fudge. It had a smooth vanilla base with chunks of chocolate fudge and a swirl of buttery caramel oozing through it. Ice cream in hand, we strolled the short five minutes down Main Street and over to the Harbor.

This time of night on the island was my favorite. The day trippers were gone for the day, and most of the overnight guests were already asleep for the night with almost everything closed. The only people out were typically locals, workers, and the few guests who opted to stay at the bars until closing. We had the sidewalk to ourselves and everything was still as we approached the harbor.

"So, Cornell. Are you excited?" Eric's eyes widened in the moonlight as we made our way to the end of the wooden docks.

"Definitely. This summer has been great, but I am lowkey exhausted and ready to be at school."

We sat down, dangling our feet over the edge as I said a silent thank you to my rushed self for not wearing flip-flops. With the amount I was fidgeting, they would surely be floating away in the lake. Looking down at my sneakers in appreciation, I noticed they were scuffed again despite me cleaning them every other day. This island made it impossible to keep anything clean.

"I feel that. My dad has been on my case all summer about choosing a major, planning what's next, and all I want to do is enjoy the last few weeks I have to play hockey."

"Are you going to miss it?" I already knew he was.

"Yeah, but it's not like I could ever play professionally so it makes sense to stop now. Besides, once I do pick a major I am sure school will be insane, and the idea of juggling both, well... it would probably have me working as hard as you are now," he chuckled.

"Very fair. Would not recommend it," I shook my head, giggling and freezing this moment in my mind.

I always wondered what it would be like to spend time together, just the two of us, and it turns out we have a lot in common. The conversation flowed so easily that I almost didn't realize when 12:30 rolled around.

"Shoot. I hate to cut this short, but I really need to go to bed if I have any hope of functioning tomorrow." How much did I really need to sleep?

"Totally. Do you have time tomorrow?"

My mind raced through my schedule for the following day while my eyes stayed locked with his, forgetting to blink. How could I consider saying no to him after all these years? Of course, I would figure out a way to make time tomorrow. We decided to do the same thing after closing the next night and finally managed to break eye contact long enough for him to walk me back to the apartment.

———

I SPENT the whole day eager to see Eric again. It was so much fun hanging out with someone who knew me. Someone who was my age, knew where I came from, and was about to embark on almost the same journey as me in the fall. He was familiar, and with everything going on with work, it was nice to fully relax and feel like I could just be myself. The crazy part was that it was Eric of all people had that effect on me. Historically his presence had made me do the opposite of relax...

That night, we grabbed a pizza from Island Slice and took it down to the harbor docks. We stayed out there laughing, gossiping about people from our high school that he had bumped into this summer, and what his friends were doing in the fall. It felt like we had been friends since we were ten years old, and I guess in some ways we had. There is something about a parallel shared history that bonds people together, even when there were limited intersections in the past.

When 12:30 AM rolled around again, going home to sleep was far from my mind. I could stay later and function on four hours, right? Eric understood though, and walked me home again, even though that meant walking straight past the Hotel Waldenwood only to have to walk back immediately after.

Maybe some of the boys from high school deserved more credit than I had given them...

———

THE NEXT NIGHT, I changed as quickly as possible, throwing on casual jeans and a striped chunky sweater to fend off the chill in the air. Bouncing through the alley around the side of the apartment, I was surprised to find Eric was not the only one waiting for me.

"George."

"Hey, Ella. I wanted to see if you wanted to come over to the Purple House tonight. Some of us are hanging; it's low key and you could leave by midnight if you need to rest." Confusion plastered across his face as he looked at Eric, "But it seems like you might have other plans?"

Great. Another last-minute invitation to a group hang. We were really still doing that?

"George this is Eric, Eric... George," I awkwardly introduced them.

"I'd be down to go meet your friends, Ellie," Eric used my middle school nickname, and I had a sneaking suspicion that he was doing that to make sure George knew that we were old friends—even if he had never called me Ellie before.

"Then I guess we should get going," I forged enthusiasm while simultaneously bracing for the awkwardness that was bound to ensue.

We walked as a group toward the Purple House while the boys asked each other surface-level questions. Most came from a necessity to play like they were getting along, while others seemed to be attempts at getting more information on each situationship. They were both trying to figure out what the other meant to me, but the joke was on them. I had no idea either.

"Can you believe this is the first party we've been to together?" Eric bumped my shoulder with his as I sunk the last cup in a round of one-on-one pong. "I tried to get you to come to one at my house junior year, but you didn't seem interested."

"What are you talking about? Of course, I would have been interested."

I would have been interested, right? I hadn't really gone to many of those parties, but that was because no one like Eric invited me. If I knew he wanted me there, I definitely would have made myself available.

"No, I don't think so. I asked at the end of one of the group meetings, and you said you had plans with Mara." Had he really asked me out and I didn't even realize it? "I felt way too rejected to try again after that, but I'm so glad I got to see you these last few days."

"Me too."

All this time, he had felt rejected by me, and I had felt the same about him. We were ships passing in the night on slightly different paths, wistfully unaware that at any moment we could have collided. I wanted to tell him how I wished he wasn't leaving tomorrow, and how I should've come to his party junior year, but George was idling very close by with an expression that had me bite my tongue before elaborating. When did I become the girl who was interested in two people? And not just any two people, two people who both knew I existed, too?

To everyone's benefit, my bedtime rolled around before anything could get too uncomfortable. George, self-aware enough to realize he could not hover forever, left Eric to walk me home.

"So, will you be back home at all before school?" Eric asked as we loitered on the sidewalk in front of the fudge shop.

"Only for a few days."

"That's too bad. Text me over Thanksgiving, okay?"

"Totally," I said while meeting him halfway for a tight hug.

Should I say anything else? Thanksgiving was a while away, maybe I should make a move? Even through the warm embrace, George's face, standing at the sideline of our pong game, floated through my head and stopped me. I let go and walked away.

Once I was alone, my brain kicked into full over-analysis mode. Had I always had a chance with Eric? Was I actually an outsider in high school or had I just opted out of experiences on my own accord? If I'd shown up to the parties and school events, would we have realized how much we had in common sooner?

I convinced myself that it didn't matter now. He'd be checking out tomorrow, and we would be moving to different schools in the fall. Although, Boston and Ithaca were not that far away from each other. Certainly closer than London and Ithaca...

———

AFTER THE WORLD'S longest closing shift which consisted of a million ice cream orders, I was ready to call it a night. Eric was gone, and I'd barely spoken to George all week other than the night at The Bridge Bar and the incredibly awkward triple date we stumbled into last night.

I barreled up the stairs counting my lot of tips for the night—$45. I'm not sure what it is about ice cream compared to fudge, but people always tip when I am working the ice cream case and rarely at the fudge counter. This was the most I had received in one night to date. *Nice.*

Channeling a character from one of my favorite shows to rewatch, I stuffed the cash in a drawer under a layer of salt-water taffy. Our doors were never locked, but I figured if this tactic was enough to fool an overbearing mother from snooping, it would certainly fool anyone who stumbled into our apartment.

"Hey," I slammed the drawer shut and spun around to see George standing in my doorway.

"Hey." Was he going to make a habit of sneaking up on me in my room?

"Did your friend leave?"

"Yeah, I checked his family out this morning. He's probably already back in Ann Arbor by now." Did he come to see me or was he just here to fish for information again?

"Cool," his eyes flickered down to his shoes. "Are you doing anything tonight?"

"Honestly, I'm exhausted. I've been working doubles for a week now, and just need to get a solid night's sleep."

The new hours were already making it tougher to see all my friends, and I couldn't keep trying to squeeze everything I wanted to do into the hours of 11 PM to 1 AM night after night. After my evening rendezvous with Eric, I needed whatever measly sleep I could manage tonight. I knew I should rally, especially considering I had just come to terms with all the things I had kept myself from in high school, but I could do that tomorrow. Tonight, I could be a victim of my own actions one more time.

"Yeah, totally I get that. Would you want to go out on a date with me when you have a free night? I miss you."

At that moment, I didn't care if he only realized he missed me because someone else wanted me. This was it. He was finally, actually, truly, fully, intentionally making a plan with me. Not a last-minute bike ride because we both happen to be free or conversations off to the side of a party with all of our roommates and coworkers steps away. Not a promise that he wanted to hang out alone sometime without calling it a date or any follow-up to actually make it happen. A real, just me and him, one-on-one date. My heart felt like it could burst out of my chest and do a happy dance all the way around my teeny, tiny bedroom.

"I'd love that. Next week. Let's do it."

FIFTEEN

Mackinac Island Travel Tip #15:
The rocks are a must-see.

TWO WEEKS HAD GONE by since I started at the Hotel Waldenwood, and I hadn't had a full day off. Promises had been made that my schedule would be worked out to have one full day off per week, but in the busy season that couldn't be guaranteed.

I'd never been so tired in my life. I was starting to wonder how my shoes were holding up and fantasized about quitting, packing my bags, and leaving the island. It was one of the most beautiful places in the world, and all I wanted was to leave. Leave the island, and take a big long nap in a big beautiful bed.

It wasn't like I wasn't still enjoying the island. On days when I worked just one job, I was still going on bike rides and trying to see everyone. I'd had fun hanging out at the harbor when Eric was here, and I had a to-be-determined date coming up with George, but I knew I needed a day—just one full day —to reset.

My parents had also been wanting to visit, begging for me

to share when I'd have my next day off with them so they could make plans. This weekend in particular was good for them, so I decided to put on my big girl pants and forge against my people-pleasing nature to make the ask.

Embarrassed when they realized they'd forgotten to give me any real time off, Violet and Dorothea both promised two consecutive days off this weekend to make up for the two I had missed so far. An entire weekend off was unheard of but perfect for my family to visit.

"Oh my gosh! You'll have the whole weekend for us?" my mom gushed into the phone. "I'm already packing the car! See you tomorrow."

———

I NEVER THOUGHT SLEEPING in until 8:30 in the morning would feel like such a luxury, but it was delightful. My family wouldn't be arriving for another two hours, so I lazily got out of bed and walked down the street to our sister fudge shop for a fancy coffee.

"Ella, what are you doing here? It's your day off. Go enjoy it!!" Violet clearly still felt bad.

"I will, I will! But first, I do need some coffee."

I hoped she wouldn't feel bad for too long. Taking both jobs had been my choice, not that I could've ever said no when Inez asked me to, but she was the one getting the shortest end of the stick in the arrangement.

"Well, that we can do. I'll make you the best one." She hastily crafted me a coffee that could hardly be labeled coffee —a caramel mocha frappe with whipped cream and fresh fudge shavings on top.

"You're right. This is definitely the best one."

I happily sipped my dessert which was parading as coffee and went home to clean up before my family arrived. They were going to be staying at a little inn on the island, their trip was too last minute to get a room at the Hotel Waldenwood, but while there was nothing I could do about Tory's mess, I wanted my things to be tidy (or at least tidier) if they came by the apartment.

MOM
We're checking in

ABIGAIL
You better be ready

DAD
Hi, honey

ELLA
Be right there!!

I practically sprinted to the Hummingbird Inn, eager to see my family and spend the day showing them all my favorite parts of the island, many of which I hadn't visited in weeks. When I arrived, they were all checked in and waiting for me. My heart flooded with feelings of home. Mom, Dad, and Abigail.

"You guys ready to do some exploring?" I burst through the door to their purple room at the Inn.

The room was decorated with antiques and the designer had taken every opportunity possible to incorporate lilac, an over-the-top homage to the island's featured flower.

"YES!" My older sister Abigail was 21 and had been spending the summer at home working a remote computer programming internship. Our younger brother, Jeremy, was at a summer camp in Pennsylvania for the whole summer, so she was practically an only child and was as in need of this weekend as I was.

"Perfect, we can go rent some bikes for you guys and grab mine."

Within 20 minutes we were off on our way on a ride around the island. I was careful to stop at all the key spots to point out arch rock, the lighthouse, and, of course, the Mackinac Bridge.

When we were almost all the way around, I turned us up off the main loop and toward the Grand Hotel. We had to pause halfway up the hill for my family to walk their bikes, but I had grown used to it on my many rides visiting the horses in the bluffs. We grabbed ice cream cones from Sadie's Ice Cream Parlor and then snuck out onto the front porch. It is usually $10 per person to get on the grounds, but I knew the secret. If you buy ice cream first, you can just walk right on by as if you're staying there.

"So, Ellie. Tell us, what's it like working so hard?" My dad was quite proud that I had been keeping up this schedule and would be saving so much before college.

"It's honestly brutal but worth it. The hardest part is just keeping up with everyone else socially. They all work half the hours but expect me to still be around to hang out every night. I'm also younger than a lot of them, which doesn't help. By the time I'm free a lot of nights, most people have already left for the bars."

"Well, it'll all be worth it. You know, Abigail, you could learn a thing or two from your sister's work ethic. You know I've caught you watching Netflix in the middle of your 'workday' one too many times," Mom chimed in.

Mom worked four days a week in a women's health clinic, so she was home during the day to see Abigail working the other day.

"Mom. It's literally fine. Everyone does it when they work remotely," she huffed and rolled her eyes, undoubtedly sick of having this conversation. "Either way though, I'm proud of you, little Ellie. Now you just need to introduce me to all your friends tonight!"

"Hey now, we have plans for a family dinner first," Dad faked feeling left out by the idea of us going off without them.

And an amazing dinner it was. We went to The Woods, the restaurant out in the woods and up by the golf course. It was the same one I had gone to with George after we went bike riding earlier in the summer, but we had only had Diet Coke and free popcorn that day, so I was thrilled to try the actual food.

After a huge meal, my parents claimed to be ready to turn in. Abigail and I knew them better though; they were going to let us go have our fun while they went to another bar to have their own date night.

"Ellie. I am SO excited to finally meet your friends. I can't wait to meet Emma and, of course, Georgeeee," Abigail squealed.

"Please don't embarrass me. Things have still gone nowhere with George, but he finally asked me out on a real date," I pleaded.

"Me? Embarrass you? I could never." She skipped along the sidewalk giggling gleefully, no doubt thinking about all the ways she had embarrassed me in the past.

We both knew she could and probably would, again.

"Well, this is it," I waved to the Purple House, buying some time before we entered.

My stomach sank as I mentally prepared for whatever scenario would come next. I was thrilled to be with Abigail, but introducing her to my friends? Well, they would be thrilled to see her too. Which meant, they would later be less thrilled to see me. People always liked her more.

"Should we have brought something?" Abigail was suddenly worried, her calm demeanor faded, and at that moment it was obvious we were sisters.

Both people pleasers and worriers although she usually wore it with more confidence.

"Actually, yeah. I forgot that we could bring something this time! Good call. Let's go to the store."

We walked back over to the store so she could grab a case of seltzers.

"Take two," I whispered under my breath as we walked into the house.

Within ten minutes, Abigail had won everyone over as expected. Jack and one of the fudge makers looked ready to throw hands over who would get to talk with her the most, and she had already told Emma she was going to visit her in Wales next year.

While Abigail held court in the kitchen, I took some time to catch up with George, and he asked about Eric. Again. And I assured him that nothing was happening. Again.

Although, Eric had been texting me every day since his family's visit...

"So when are you going to take my sister out?" Kitchen court was out of session, and Abigail had moved on to her next defendant.

My cheeks flushed, and I was suddenly grateful to have so many hot, sweaty bodies in one room to disguise my embarrassment.

"I hope soon. I'm just waiting for her to have time for me in her busy schedule," George was overtly pleased that he had already asked and could punt the question back to me.

"You'll know when I'm free as soon as I do! Tuesday night seems promising though."

"I'll be waiting by the phone," he drummed his fingers across his cell phone screen in that ASMR way and my stomach did a somersault, grateful to no longer be the one waiting.

Shortly after Abigail's confrontation with George, we said our goodbyes and I dropped her off at the Inn before heading back to my apartment. I was floundering back and forth between not believing she would embarrass me like that and kicking myself for ever thinking otherwise.

———

SUNDAY MORNING, we woke up early to get in line for the best breakfast on the island, The Boot. It was a tiny diner, no bigger than a postage stamp, and it had a cowboy theme. The walls were covered in cowboy hats and prints. When you think about it too long, it makes zero sense that it's located right in the heart of Main Street in a resort town in northern Michigan, but somehow in reality it fits in perfectly. No trip to the island would be complete without their breakfast burrito.

"Okay fine, I forgive you for waking us up early for this." Abigail was hungover and devouring her food. "This is the biggest and bestest burrito I have ever had."

"Why don't you try to finish chewing before talking?" I rolled my eyes, still annoyed about last night. I tried to slide farther away from her in the sticky red diner booth.

"What? You don't want to see this?" She opened her mouth and showed all of us the mix of the eggs, bacon, cheese, salsa, and tortilla that she was enjoying so very much.

"Okay, enough. I know you had a little too much fun last night, but let's pretend to all be adults here." My mom hated to lay down the law, but chewing with your mouth open was a big no-no. "Anyway, what did you have in mind for today, Ariella?"

"I thought we could go to Sugar Loaf Rock. I haven't actually biked up there myself yet this summer, but everyone says it's worth checking out."

They'd already seen a lot of the island, so biking farther into the State Park was as good as any activity to squeeze in between eating breakfast, lunch, and fudge.

An hour later, we managed to find our way to the rock. Sugar Loaf was a tall skinny rock that towered over 70 feet tall. Standing in front of it, it was hard to believe that it wasn't man-made and actually just eroded into the statue-like form that it is today. From there, we made our way over to Arch Rock and took the obligatory photos, enjoying the way it perfectly framed the dazzling blue water below.

Following the rocks, I took them to lunch at the restaurant in Hotel Waldenwood. We were treated like royalty with a table right on the water. I had watched this table from the front desk, enjoying the view of the restaurant crowd when the lobby was slow, but this was my first time eating here. The seahorse details in the lobby had extended into the restaurant, with cute cartoons printed on the cups and embroidered into the napkins. Each detail perfectly planned. Even the white tablecloth cascaded into my lap like a little blanket, fending off the afternoon breeze.

"What next? Should we go get some fudge before we have to head home?" Mom was so excited to be seeing everywhere I worked, and I think she wished she could have taken the summer off from her own job to work up here with me.

My mom had worked at summer camps growing up, which was fairly typical for a teen from the suburbs of New York, but she had never worked anywhere quite like this. I was glad she could at least experience it secondhand through my stories and this weekend.

"Yeah, let's do it."

The shop was packed to the brim with fudgies. It was the third week of July, and peak season was in session.

"Ella! Abigail! Can I help you?" Emma called from behind the counter, excited to have a break from the demands of tourists and help us instead.

"Yes, thank you! Mom, Dad, what do you guys want to take home?"

They quickly gave their order and gushed over the fact that they didn't need to pay. Mom handed Emma $20, feeling like it was the least she could do after getting so much fudge for free. Emma took it reluctantly and whispered that she would save it to buy us drinks when she turned 21 in a couple of weeks.

With their suitcases packed, and their extra bags of fudge in hand, I walked my family down to the ferry dock. It was a slow walk with a few pit stops into the souvenir stores along the way. My mom desperately wanted to buy me a Mackinac Island sweatshirt, and somehow our family ended up all buying matching ones. It would have been embarrassing if they weren't about to all get on a boat and not return until summer was over. A small part of me wished I was going with them.

"Bye, Ellie. Thanks for letting me steal all your friends last night." Abigail smothered me in a tight hug, jostling my wavy brown hair.

"Bye, honey." Dad's hug was quicker and looser.

"I'll be back to pick you up next month! You have so much fun, but not too much fun, and be safe until then." My mom's hug was the longest.

Bags in hand, they walked along the small metal bridge between the dock and the ferry. One by one, they boarded the boat. I stayed for a few minutes, watching them climb to the top deck, and then took off back toward my apartment once the ferry had pulled out of view.

SIXTEEN

**Mackinac Island Travel Tip #16:
Order ice cream every night.**

WITH A WHOLE FREE evening ahead of me, I figured it was time to cash in on this date with George. I quickly texted to confirm he would be free tonight, and just two minutes later he responded with a full plan.

I apprehensively biked over to the glow golf course, palms sweating against the rubber handlebars of my bike. This was my first proper date with George—the other times we had spent time together it had been an add-on to another plan with the group, but this was an intentional date. I wiped my palms on the back of my jean shorts. *You got this.* I walked over to George who was standing by the first hole holding two putters and two glowing golf balls. He'd gotten there early. That was a good sign.

"Hey! I got you a pink one since it's your favorite color."

It was a statement, not a question—he remembered my favorite color. I swayed in the breeze, nervously avoiding eye contact as I took the ball from him.

"Awesome, thank you! This is cool. I've never seen a putt-putt course like this."

I scanned the course filled with natural grass greens, mini sandtraps, and lots of lumps and bumps. It sprawled over a peninsula, inching close to the water and giving every hole a sweeping view of Lake Huron.

"I know, it's very posh, and honestly I am glad that I won't need to try to avoid any crazy windmills or tricks. You want to go first?" George looked a little nervous too.

I laid my ball down behind the glowing line and swung softly. "I guess I should've let you go first to see how slow these greens are." My nose crinkled as I tried to make it seem cute that my putt had stopped less than halfway to the hole. Whoops.

My eyes followed George as he walked across the green, squatting down next to the hole. "Don't worry, I am sure I will be equally rubbish." I really loved when he used British words...

"Hey! That's cheating. You can't go look from the other side of the hole before putting," I playfully shoved his shoulder when he returned to my side at the bottom of the green.

"Oh, yes I can. It's called reading the greens, and I have no shot of getting it in otherwise," George scoffed.

"If you insist on doing that, can you at least tell me what you're doing? I read books, not greens."

"Come here," he called me over to the far end of the hole. "You want to position yourself just behind the cup from where you start and get low." He moved my hips into position and then pulled us both down, crouched over the hole. I mimicked his movements crouching down, and, like every hopelessly romantic teenager to be in this position before me, my skin reacted warmly to his touch, his musky cologne filling my senses. "Once you're in position you look at all the curves and hills on the course and guess which way you think the ball will roll. Easy peasy."

George walked back to the base of the green and putted, putting the ball within one foot of the hole, "If you fancy, you can take a mulligan."

Oh, I fancy. I picked my ball up, lining it up at the start again. Mimicking the movements he'd just made, I pulled back and followed through. The ball came to a stop only marginally closer to the hole. "This might be a long round."

"I've got all night," George hummed, positioning himself behind me as I lined up for the next putt. "A little to the left. Nice and easy," he whispered in my ear.

By the end of the round, all of my nerves had subsided, and we were both laughing hysterically at every swing. Even if there were no trick statutes, the greens were tougher than any putt-putt course I'd played before, with random hills and turns. As much as I was trying to read the greens, I would've had more luck reading through the encyclopedia. The shadows of the night sky made it impossible to see the bumps and it was taking both of us five to seven strokes per hole.

"Well, that was way harder than expected. Want to drown our sorrows in ice cream?" George asked.

"Always."

We walked to the "pro shop," even though Rosanna's was still open, and we could get as much free ice cream as we wanted there. The money didn't matter as much as the implication that he didn't want the date to end, which it inevitably would have if we went back into the center of town.

Ice cream cones in hand, we strolled through the course again until we came to a little bench overlooking the water. The lights were twinkling on top of the Round Island Lighthouse across the way, but the rest of the water was still and dark with only the moon and the stars shining. The silence was almost tangible in the air, both our bodies drawn together on the bench like opposite ends of a magnet.

"So, how are things going with the hotel? You feel okay about the schedule?"

"Yeah, it's awesome being over there. Definitely, a lot to learn still, but I love talking to the guests and helping them see the magic of the island. I get to know them a lot better there than at the fudge shop. This weekend we have a huge yacht race coming, and I can't wait to be fully booked. Everyone says it is the best weekend of the year." I uncrossed my legs and faced George on the bench, my breath catching in my throat as I realized just how close together we had slid.

"Yeah, that seems awesome. We are preparing for the rush too," George agreed. "Have you ever been on a yacht?"

"Is that a serious question?" I chortled. "When would I have been on a yacht?"

"I don't know. It comes up sometimes," George flinched, leaning forward with his elbows on his knees.

"Oh my god. You've totally been on a yacht," I laughed. "Tell me everything."

We carried on for a bit, the conversation naturally twisting and turning through different topics, my sides growing sore from laughing at our stories about goofy customer interactions from the last week, and any awkwardness plaguing us since Eric's visit fully dissipating.

"You have to try this," I held my cone of birthday cake-flavored ice cream out to him.

The base was vanilla with neon blue icing swirls and a rainbow of sprinkles. Until I had tried the Mackinac Island Fudge flavor at Rosanna's, this had been my absolute favorite with its artificial sugary sweetness that, for some reason, I was obsessed with.

George leaned over and—like a real heathen—took a huge bite from the side of my ice cream.

"You can't just bite into ice cream!" I gasped, trying to catch my breath from laughing so hard.

"This is repulsive," he stuck his tongue out at me.

"No, this is the best flavor... other than Mackinac Island Fudge. It's so good."

"I am seriously starting to question your taste, Ellie. That was vile."

He scooted even closer to me on the bench, closing the last little gap between us, his knees knocking into mine, and my heart pounding in my chest. It was the first time he had called me by my nickname's nickname, and I was suddenly very aware of the sound of my own breathing.

"Maybe I should take a second bite just to make sure."

As George leaned in for a second bite, he rerouted from my sticky sweet ice cream and suddenly his lips were on mine, still sugary with a thin coating of birthday cake ice cream. He may have complained, but I would savor the flavor of his mouth on mine for the rest of my life. This moment, sitting on a bench, overlooking the water while holding ice cream cones, I would always remember this night and the way the moonlight shined as he finally kissed me.

Syrupy.

Sweet.

Delicious.

"It's about time," I resisted the urge to lick my lips as we locked eyes, both of us slightly out of breath. "I was starting to think we were just friends."

"Definitely more than friends," his adorable dimple appeared on one side.

"Glad that's finally settled," I whispered as he leaned back in, my heart still racing.

We were kissing again, but this time it was slower as if the first kiss had come from a place of need and this one was coming from a place of want. Entirely different, but equally spectacular.

I had kissed boys throughout high school, and even a few in middle school, but this was different. Those kisses had been quick, stolen in a hallway or at a school dance or forced in a car after a movie because it was the thing to do.

But this kiss? I'd waited for this kiss. I'd dreamed about it, wondered what it would be like, and then felt a tingle through my whole body when it exceeded every expectation. I wanted it to happen again. I feared the day it wouldn't.

We stayed on the bench a while longer, alternating between kissing, looking out at the lake, and staring into each other's eyes. I was sure that if anyone had been watching us, they would have thought we were disgustingly cute. I felt disgustingly cute. I never wanted to feel anything but disgustingly cute ever again.

When the Sunday scaries (aka my dread for the work week ahead) plowed their way through our happy bubble, George walked me all the way home, hand-in-hand, dragging our bikes next to us, neither of us wanting to get on them to allow the night to end any sooner than necessary. This was what summer was about. Work could wait.

Despite my challenges on the course, it turned out that George was actually excellent at making plans.

SEVENTEEN

Mackinac Island Travel Tip #17:
Beware the sailors.

ALL WEEK we had been preparing for the Yacht Race to arrive on Mackinac Island, and today was the day. Hundreds of sailors (and sailor-esses) were going to ascend on the island after making the 40-to-65-hour journey from Chicago on their sailboats. The race was a tradition that had been around for over a century. I was wearing my best blue and white striped dress for the occasion, and could not wait to start checking people in and hearing their stories of the odyssey.

Around 2 PM, the chaos ensued. The first group ran in, already rowdy, and asked to check in. Within minutes of checking in, they were down at the lobby bar, celebrating and toasting their winnings. It was hard to believe they had even had time to toss the bags in their rooms, let alone shower or change after their multi-day expedition.

We were one of the closest hotels to the harbor, and practically every single guest was either part of the race or related to someone who was part of the race.

"Hey, darling. Checking in under Jacobson." Two men stood before me at the front desk, one appeared to be in his late 20s, and the other in his early 40s.

"Welcome to the Hotel Waldenwood. Please give me just one moment while I pull up your reservation."

They would be staying for two nights in a double queen room overlooking Main Street. I got their keys together while they quizzed me on everything they should do while on the island. Unlike some of the other groups, they seemed interested in more than the bar.

"Have you ever been on a sailing yacht, Ariella?" Mr. Jacobson glanced down at my name tag.

"No, but I love boats. I am sure it's spectacular to race them."

Why did people keep assuming I had been on any kind of yacht? Had I been giving yacht vibes?

"It really is," he sighed, eyes heavy as if already reminiscing on today's race.

"Don't worry. Your room will be spectacular too," I cringed at my own cheesy words, passing his keys over the desk, and watched them walk away, hoping I could come up with something better to say to the rest of the guests.

"Hi, Ella," Inez placed her perfectly manicured hands on the front desk.

"Hi, Inez. How are you today?" I made a silent wish that she had not heard my clunky interaction with the last guest.

"Good, good. It's one of my favorite times of the year!" She smiled at the crowds in the lobby. "I heard you have been doing a wonderful job over here, and I really appreciate you stepping up."

"Thank you, Inez. It is truly my pleasure. Is there anything I can help you with today?" I used my most professional voice, which was almost unrecognizable even to myself.

"Actually, I am here to see you. I want to add you to the

pool for the end-of-season bonus. I know you're leaving before the end of the season, but it only seems fair with how hard you are working."

The end-of-season bonus was notorious. Anyone who worked the full season—April through October—was eligible for a portion of any profits that exceeded the earnings from the prior summer. Most people couldn't stay the full season, but if you could, the bonus made it worth it. I had heard rumors that each person received a few thousand dollars from it last year.

"Really?"

"Of course, really," she smiled warmly. "You've earned it."

First the kiss with George and now this. This summer was turning out to be better than I ever imagined.

———

AFTER FINISHING MY CHECK-INS, I still had a full shift ahead of me at the fudge shop. Then I woke up again the next morning at 6:30 AM, dreadfully in sync with Tory, and started it all over again.

"Ariella. How are you standing here right now? Do you sleep?" My favorite racer from the hotel had come into the fudge shop late last night and had been shocked to see me working there.

And here he was again, at my desk a few hours later looking utterly disturbed to see me standing, dressed up with a smile on my face.

"I promise I do," I mustered a giggle despite feeling truly dead inside. "I even have tonight off, so from 3 PM on I am free as a bird to nap, eat, or wander the island on my bike."

I reassured him that I was very much working these hours of my own volition. Or at least on my own inability to set boundaries and desire to work the system for early college credits.

"Well, if that's the case you need to come by our boat tonight. You said you've never been on a yacht, right?" The older of the Jacobson men casually propped his elbow on the desk, looking around the room as if bored by his own question.

"My uncle loves showing off his boat. He will probably invite another 20 people to come to tour it today too," The younger Jacobson chimed in, clearly aware that I was weighing the pros of visiting a boat with the cons of being abducted at sea. Or at lake?

"In that case, that would be great. Can I bring a friend?" It was advertised as a mostly friendly invite, and I didn't want to pass up my only chance to go on a yacht, but there was definite safety in numbers.

Plus, it somehow felt more professional, although I'm not entirely sure why.

"The more the merrier. It will be yachts of fun. See you at nine." His expression transformed from its earlier boredom, exuding pride in his pun, and clearly happy with the outcome of his seemingly casual invite.

Before I could ask for details on how to find him, he wandered off, and I quickly ran through the contenders of who to join me. Emma was closing tonight and I never hung out with Sophie alone. Bringing a boy would likely ruffle feathers, so Tory was the safest option. She was also tough, so if things got weird, I could rely on her. She did promise to have my back all summer, and it was about time I collected. Besides, she owed me for always disappearing when her boyfriend visited.

Immediately after my shift, I bumped into Tory in our room. She was gushing about all the cute sailors checking into the Inn today, and I invited her to come with me that night.

"I am so down. Also, you need me there for protection," she smirked as if knowing that was exactly why I had invited her. "Don't want any men getting the wrong idea!"

"So true. Meet you back here at nine?"

We set the plans and went about our own business for the rest of the day.

———

AT A QUARTER PAST NINE, respectfully late, we wandered down into the harbor. Unsure where to start, we shuffled our way through the array of docks. There is a large chain that usually requires a key to get to this area, but it had been removed and every boat in the harbor was alive with people laughing, cheering, and toasting to the race.

Unlike the ferry docks, which each consisted of one long pier out into the water, the harbor was a maze of smaller docks protruding into the lake, allowing boats to tie up and stay awhile. A floating parking lot of oversized, and likely over-priced, adult toys.

"Ella! You came. And you brought friends," The younger guy, who I learned was named James, called from the front of one of the biggest boats.

It was a large white sailboat that appeared to be at least 30 feet long, made of wood and plexiglass; it looked like it could glide across the water completely frictionless.

"Hey! Of course, we couldn't pass up an opportunity to see what this is all about," I awkwardly waved around, unsure how to act casually about taking an old man and his nephew up on an offer to tour their racing yacht.

"Naturally," he chuckled and met us by the side of the boat. It was rocking gently, sitting about two feet above the dock. "Can I help you, ladies, up?"

We each took turns being pulled up onto the boat by

James. Once safely aboard, he gave us a very thorough tour. We started by going down a steep wooden ladder into the underside of the boat, walking through a hallway of hammock-like beds. There was a small kitchenette, two bathrooms, and a room full of tools and maps. It was the exact opposite of the glamorous yacht I was expecting, which instantly made complete sense given it was for racing and not relaxing in the Mediterranean Sea. An image of George on a mega yacht somewhere off the coast of Greece brought a small smile to my face.

From the dock, the boat had looked plenty big, but I was still awestruck by all the winding chambers underneath. This was a serious racing boat designed for sport and each room had its function. It was the kind of place I would probably never find myself again, and I was so glad I said yes to the Jacobsons.

"James, I hope you're giving them a good tour! Did he show you the maps yet?" His uncle joined us from the back room which had a proper bed and private bathroom.

"Absolutely, this boat is crazy. I can't believe you all sleep stacked up like this," I pointed to the bed hammocks, hanging loosely from the walls.

"Oh, hardly. Once we are racing there's rarely more than one or two people down here at any given time," James said, helping me back up the wooden ladder to the main level of the boat.

"Would you girls like a drink?" Mr. Jacobson asked, swishing a deep orange drink in his own hand.

"Whatever you are having would be great," I smiled, unsure what kind of drink would have been appropriate to ask for.

"Two negronis coming right up."

He mixed an array of liquids in a stainless steel cup before slapping a top on and aggressively shaking, ice knocking against the metal with each movement. I took a slow sip of the drink, which was far fancier than anything else I had tried this summer, and my face puckered. It was bitter and strong. I knew I was supposed to like it, but I couldn't understand why.

Suddenly I had a second drink in hand, and I was laughing at everything anyone said. "Land hoe!" I giggled, spinning the wheel as quickly as I could. Taking turns, Tory and I both pretended to steer the ship and tugged on the masts. It was so childish, but none of the sailors appeared to mind. If anything, James was egging it on, showing a lot of interest in Tory.

"Ella," Tory whispered, poking me in the side. "Ella, can you hear me?"

"Yes, I'm right here," I poked her back.

"Can James come back to our room tonight? You can totally stay too, but like," she paused, "you might not want to."

Tory's boyfriend had visited a few times in June, but his last visit had been weeks ago, so I shouldn't have been surprised. It's not like she would've confided in me about the change, but it did explain her foul mood last week, and I wish she would've trusted me to tell me.

"Totally. I'll go to Emma's."

The negronis were starting to go to my head, and I needed to abort this ship before I did anything that could get me in trouble at work. Anything other than fraternizing with guests on their giant yacht...

ELLA

Can we cuddle tonight?

Tory offered for me to stay but...

EMMA

Offended you would even ask

Get over here

With Tory preoccupied, I said my thank yous and good-byes, and headed for the Purple House, ready to debrief the day with Emma.

I WOKE up in the middle of the night after a dream in which I was on a boat searching for a bathroom. Unlike the boat tonight, this one didn't have any, and dream me was frantically exploring every nook and cranny. It was one of those dreams that when you wake up, you know you need to find a bathroom immediately or you just might pee yourself.

Stumbling into the dark hallway, I dragged my hands across the paint-chipped walls in a hazy effort to find the light switch. Before I detected it, the door to the bathroom swung open, a burst of light spreading out into the hall, revealing a face that I would recognize anywhere.

"Hey." My eyes darted down to my PJs, a pink and white floral set I had left at Emma's for nights like tonight.

"What are you doing here?" The corners of George's mouth sleepily crept up into a smile.

"Oh you know, sleepwalked here from the big apartment," I laughed. "No, Tory picked up a guest tonight at the harbor, so I'm bunking with Emma."

"You could've texted me. I love taking in strays." He moved closer, positioning himself just an inch from my body.

A quick shiver ran through me, the memory of our kiss still fresh in my mind, "I'll have to keep that in mind for next time."

"You think there will be a next time?"

"Respectfully, there will definitely be a next time."

I passed no judgment, only recognition. Tory would have no problem with people knowing she was living her best life this summer, exactly as she should.

"You know, you could come even if you haven't been thrown out on Main Street to sleep with the horses?" He tucked a stray strand of my wavy brown hair behind my ear, moving even closer, I noticed a muscle in his jaw twitch.

"Jack wouldn't mind?"

"He likes horses."

George closed the gap, taking me tight against his chest and kissing me softly. Want and desire had cornered me against the wall. Separating only to catch our breath, I ran my finger-tips over his cheek and dimple before tracing his lips lightly, and then we were kissing again. It was even better than the other night.

So good, that until this very moment, I had forgotten just how much I had to pee. I leaned into the kiss for a few more seconds before pulling back abruptly.

"I hate to do this, but I really did come out here for the bathroom."

"Yeah, yeah, that's what they all say," George winked before disappearing back into his room and softly closing his door as I headed for the bathroom.

I spent the next morning floating around the fudge shop, ignoring the commotion around me by replaying the previous night on a loop in my mind.

With the yacht crews in town, the fudge makers were showboating more than usual. Chanting while mixing the heavy cauldron of boiling fudge, yelling fires away while dumping the mixture onto the marble countertops, and singing as they used their paddles to form the fudge block.

People don't always realize, but making fudge is a highly labor-intensive craft. You have to be incredibly strong with high endurance, which is why most of the fudge makers on the island are men. Not because they won't allow women to make it, but because many of us ladies try it out, knowing anything men can do we can do better, and then quickly realize we are happier to be selling the fudge.

Late afternoon, my good old sailor friends showed up ready for trouble. "Ella, get in there. We want to see you make the fudge."

"But then who's going to get you your fudge?"

Sometimes when it was busy, I would go back there to help pour the cauldron so that the guys could stagger who was forming fudge across multiple tables, but I usually avoided it. My upper body strength was, and still is, nonexistent.

"You know we already have more fudge than we can eat on the journey home; we want to see you make some."

This was about to turn into full-on heckling, and as much as I had grown more outgoing throughout this summer of talking to people all day every day, I wanted to do whatever I could to avoid that.

"Fine. Kai, do you even need help over there?" He was my favorite fudge maker and the only one I regularly helped.

"From you? Never, but come on over," Kai laughed, quickly spinning a stainless steel paddle around in the copper cauldron over the fire. "Alright folks, we are now going to be pouring a batch of one of our bestsellers, Oreo. My assistant, Ella, will be helping me. Now, this is very hot and very heavy, so you might want to back up. She's a little clumsy."

He turned his attention to the crowd, throwing an exaggerated wink in their direction, always happy to put on a show for his adoring fans. Parents started to pull their kids back a little from the white picket fence that separated the marble fudge tables from the rest of the shop.

We both lifted together, Kai clearly taking the majority of the 150 pounds of fudge and copper. Pouring slowly, my muscles tightened as the chocolate spilled over the edge of the cauldron and filled the marble to the silver stoppers that were placed around the edges of the table.

"So folks, we let this sit for a minute. The marble table will work its magic, cooling the fudge. Once it's no longer runny, I'll remove these silver edges and start to work the fudge with my paddle for about 15 minutes. That's what makes our fudge the smoothest on the island. It cools gradually on the table as we constantly move it," Kai continued his show as I retreated to my station behind the counter.

The Jacobsons decided to buy more despite their haul from earlier in the weekend, and after paying with a credit card slid me a $20 bill.

For the second time that summer, I caught myself thinking that the most unexpected friendships really do turn out to be the most fruitful.

EIGHTEEN

Mackinac Island Travel Tip #18:
Book a hotel with a jacuzzi.

TONIGHT WAS GOING to be a big night, and, like the angel she is, Marlani let me leave a little early from work while she closed out. Emma was turning 21 tonight, and everyone was planning to gather at the Purple House to celebrate before going to one of the fancier bars at the Grand Hotel. The cocktails there were usually too expensive for our group, but everyone (except me) was willing to splurge a little for our favorite lady from Wales.

Walking up the front porch, I smoothed my dress, a pastel yellow cotton with little white daisies embroidered on it. My mom had gotten it for me at one of the boutiques on Main Street during their visit, and this seemed like the perfect occasion, even if I couldn't join everyone at the bar at midnight.

"Are the rumors true?" Jared grabbed my arm as soon as I walked through the door. "Are you actually so stupid you went on one of the yachts this week?"

"The first part is, but it was hardly a stupid thing to do. Have you seen those boats?"

"If I knew you were so desperate to go on a boat, I would've just invited you on mine. You know I have one on the dock right behind your apartment, and you could confidently get on it knowing I'm not an ax murderer."

"You know what's sad? I'm not sure if I'd be that confident in that."

I searched the room for George, not wanting to spend too long talking to Jared who was impossible not to fall into a flirty banter with. As my eyes scanned the worn-down furniture and familiar faces, my belly warmed with how much of a place I had made for myself on this little island. Comfortable. Flirty. Even a little reckless.

George was playing beer pong with Jack against Andre and Chase and didn't seem to be making any moves to exit the game. I thought we had left this aloof behavior on the first hole of the golf course.

"How's the birthday going, Emma?" I turned my attention to the star of the show, swallowing my frustrations.

"So good! It's funny because twenty-one isn't even a big birthday at home, but everyone is making such a big deal. It's amazing—like a repeat of my eighteenth." She sipped her bright pink cocktail, twirling around the living room in a feather boa that I had given her for the occasion.

"Wait, I love that. It's like a free second chance birthday," I grabbed my cocktail and spun around the room with her, delighted to be a part of her special day.

"Exactly! I spent my eighteenth at a club in Cardiff, but this living room is better," she giggled, glancing at all of our friends who filled the room with so much love and joy.

Someone had set up streamers, I had brought party hats for everyone, and there was a huge 'cake' made of stacked fudge slices in the corner. It was quite the scene.

As midnight crept closer and people started to make moves to go to the bar, my earlier frustrations were creeping back up. George might still be acting the same as he had in June, but that didn't mean I had to. I was done waiting around.

"Ella, where are you going?" George cut in front of me as the group descended the front porch steps.

"Um, I was going to go home?" I figured I'd walk with everyone and veer off to the apartment, salvaging the evening by getting a full(ish) night's sleep.

"Oh, I actually thought I'd hang back too, and we could do something. How do you feel about a night swim?" The moon twinkled, brightening his face enough for me to see the mischievous look in his eye.

He had something specific in mind.

"You know the lake will be like 30 degrees right now?"

"You mean 0. You Americans are so funny with your unique systems; Celsius is good enough for the rest of the world. Anyway, yes, I know it's too cold in the lake. A mate of mine works over at the Isle Manor and said I could use the pool anytime it's closed. Which is now."

I could go home now. He had been cold to me all night, and he deserved it. But I also deserved to have a fun night, and staying was what would salvage it for me. In a way choosing him was choosing me.

Following George's lead, we walked through the backyard of the Isle Manor until we came to a greenhouse at the far end of the property that housed an indoor swimming pool and jacuzzi. Sure enough, a guy in an Isle Manor t-shirt came to let us in and even handed us plush lavender-scented towels.

"He owes me because I always sneak him extra fries," George whispered as he discarded his shirt onto one of the white and green striped lounge chairs. I averted my eyes, not wanting to be caught staring at his now shirtless abs, and took off my shoes, plopping them under the same chair. "Ready?"

"Wait, I didn't even think this through. I don't have a swimsuit."

"Easy fix." George came closer, tugging gently on the hem of my daisy dress. "This looks waterproof."

"It's not." I bashfully took off the dress, grateful that I had worn a nice pair of underwear, always cognizant that my dress could blow up in the late night wind while biking, and a matching bra. I wondered if he noticed.

One look at his expression, and I was certain he had.

Reaching for my hand, we walked in lockstep to the edge of the pool. Looking into each other's eyes, we counted down in our heads, reading one another's thoughts, before jumping into the deep end.

Submerged underwater, I paused, holding my breath tight in my chest and wanting to remember the feeling of being grounded underwater in my underwear while trespassing in a hotel pool. Breaking the surface, I gulped for air, refilling my lungs before rejoining George in a tangle of limbs under the water. None of my friends from home would believe it. It was completely unlike me to do something like this, and yet it felt right as if I'd been this fun and spontaneous in my last life.

"This is perfect." George spun me around in the lukewarm water, my legs wrapped tightly around his bare torso. I pressed my face into his neck, holding him close. He brushed my wild hair out of my face and kissed me, electricity coursing through my lips and freezing time.

A while later, we both leaned back in the pool, tilting our heads toward the sky and staring out the greenhouse ceiling to the stars.

"I think that's the Big Dipper," I pointed up.

"I think you're right." His entire face was glowing, not even looking to see where I was pointing.

"You didn't even look!" I playfully splashed him.

"Didn't need to. I trust you."

My heart sank into the pit of my stomach, that simple phrase in that simple moment solidifying that the end of the summer was going to rip my heart out and tear it to shreds, one way or another.

NINETEEN

Mackinac Island Travel Tip #19:
Embrace Island Time and never set an alarm.

WHAT'S GOING ON? My head throbbed as I rubbed my puffy eyes. My memory of the night before came back to me in a rush of crushed tall skinny cans and triangles of red cups. The pong tournament. After seven grueling rounds, my team had achieved a sweet victory.

I reached over to my phone on the nightstand only to find it dead. In my hazy state, I must have forgotten to plug it in. I hung over the edge of the bed, fingertips grazing the floor as they searched for my charger. *Where was Tory?*

"Oh my god," I whispered to the empty room. "What time is it?!"

10:13 AM flashed on the screen as my phone resurrected itself. My shift at the hotel had started three hours ago, and Tory hadn't bothered to wake me up on her way out.

I sprung into action, clothes flying across the room as I slammed my dresser drawers. I could still make it. The morning could have been slow. All was not lost. In a scramble,

I pulled on a skirt and blouse combo and quickly ran a dry toothbrush through my mouth once before stumbling my way down the stairs to the road.

I practically sprinted through the early birds who were leisurely strolling down Main Street, trying to enjoy a slow start to their mornings, only to be disturbed by me. As I ran through the door to Hotel Waldenwood, I smoothed out my skirt and tried to catch my breath.

"Dorothea. Hi, I'm so sorry I'm late," I walked briskly, joining her behind the front desk.

"I'm glad you're okay," she stared forward, not turning to look at me head-on. "When I got the call at ten past seven that you were a no-show, I thought 'No, that couldn't be right. Ella wouldn't do that unless something was seriously wrong.' But here you are. You've missed almost half of your shift and your shirt is on inside out."

My hands instantly sprang to the back collar of my shirt. The tag was sticking out, announcing to the world that I was a size M at LOFT.

"I'm so sorry. It will ne—"

"Go home. I'm finishing your shift for the rest of the day," she cut me off. "I would recommend you shower before showing up at Rosanna's this afternoon."

"Okay," I looked down at my feet, all too aware that she still hadn't looked at me straight on. "I promise it will never happen again. I am so sorry that you had to cover for me."

I made my way back to the apartment much slower. My back hunched over in shame, feet barely coming off the pavement with each step. My shirt was still on inside out, but I didn't care who saw it. This was a new low, and I deserved any ridicule that came my way.

I had always been someone people could rely on. *Ariella Abrams, she might not be the funniest or the most beautiful, but she was smart and reliable. You could count on that girl in a crisis.* I liked to think that was how people perceived me. Someone who showed up when and where they were expected, and never let their phone die after an evening of being splashed by ping pong balls landing in sticky liquids while someone played Eminem over living room speakers.

After all the hours, and the sacrifices to balance both jobs, I had blown it in one night. I proved I couldn't keep up or be counted on. I collapsed back in my bed, disappointed in myself with no clue how to salvage the situation. *Would I even still be eligible for the end-of-season bonus?*

By the time my afternoon shift rolled around, I had cleaned myself off and prepared a game plan to grovel to Dorothea tomorrow morning. I'd show up 30 minutes early to work, charm the night guy who must have stayed late this morning in my absence, and then charm her.

"Ella, can you please come out back to chat before you start," Violet's voice chimed from behind me as I clocked in.

"Of course," I followed her outside to the picnic table where Inez and Dorothea were already waiting for us.

"I can assume you know why we are all here," Inez started with a serious expression on her face.

"I am so sor—" My apology was cut off for the second time that day.

"I am sorry we put you in this position," Inez continued. "I know you're only eighteen and it was too much for us to expect you to take on both jobs while still enjoying your summer on the island. I should have realized it wouldn't work before we offered, but I knew you wanted the credits, and we were in a jam."

"I can handle it. I know I messed up this morning, and I am so sorry for inconveniencing everyone and letting you down, but I promise it won't happen again," I let the groveling commence.

"Are you sure you still want to do both jobs?" Inez asked,

Dorothea and Violet both looking at me with kind understanding in their eyes. "We can try to figure out a solution to lighten the load if not."

"Yes, I want to do both jobs. I love both and am getting different things out of each. You don't need to change a thing. I will be more responsible," I assured the group, stretching my back tall and straight as if good posture would prove I could handle anything.

"Okay," Inez paused to take a deep breath, "You have a little over a month left, so you let us know if it gets to be too much."

"I will, but please know how seriously I take this. I won't let you down again," I nodded eagerly, grateful they were going to give me a second chance to prove myself.

They were truly the best bosses in the history of the world, and I hated that I had let them down. That I had given them a reason to double my competence and dedication.

"I do have one idea," Dorothea spoke up for the first time. "Why don't we move you down to four days a week at the hotel? I can make it work with the rest of the team, and it will put you at only three days of doubles per week."

"Perfect. It's settled," Inez dismissed us, and I ran inside the fudge shop, now late for a shift for the second time today.

The solution was a good one, and I would be grateful to have one fewer shift in my week, but there was still a nagging voice telling me I had failed. That I had shifted my focus too much to things that didn't matter when the work was what brought me to the island in the first place.

I pushed the voice aside and greeted my first customer of the day, determined to show Violet that I was still at my best.

TWENTY

Mackinac Island Travel Tip #20:
Plan ahead and make advance reservations. Hotels and
inns book up in peak season.

EVER SINCE OUR forbidden swim we spent each evening together, cuddling in George's twin-sized bed at the Purple House until I made my way back to my bed to sleep where I belonged, perched above Rosanna's and ready for the next day.

That night, Jack conveniently stayed over with a girl who worked in a rival fudge shop, and it would be our first full night together. Alone. Unfortunately, I still had a full shift at the hotel standing between me and our evening.

"Hello, checking in please," a man along with his wife and two kids sauntered up to the front desk. "We'd like a room with a view of the lake."

"Wonderful. What is the last name on the reservation?" Given the size of our hotel, views needed to be selected when making a booking, but I figured I would wait and see if he'd booked the correct type before letting him down easily.

"No reservation. We decided we wanted to stay here instead of using our hotel points over in Mackinaw City tonight. One room, two beds, and a lake view," he aggressively slid his credit card across the marble countertop.

"My sincere apologies, sir. We are fully booked tonight; however, I can call a few of our sister hotels to see if they have availability," I emptily offered, knowing very well that every similar hotel was sold out tonight as well.

"No, we want a lake view. I'll pay more than your rack rate."

"Unfortunately, that's not something we do here. Can I call around and try to find another option for you?"

At this point, he was giving me an incredibly nasty look. My dad always told me to *never let someone else's lack of planning become your emergency* but working in a hotel, where the guest is always right, that happens daily.

"No. If you can't figure out how to make it work for us here, how could I trust you to help?" he barked at me. His wife turned slightly red as she tried to distract their children, clearly hoping that they would not notice how harsh and unkind their father was to people who were only trying to help him fix his own mistakes. "We came all the way here, and this is the only hotel directly on the water. You understand that, right?"

My face flushed red, feeling guilty for the mistake I hadn't made.

"Of course. Unfortunately, this is the peak season for us so we are unable to accommodate walk-ins. My family recently stayed at the Hummingbird Inn, and it's a wonderful option for last-minute bookings," I subtly reiterated that he had no reservation, attempting to shield myself from the other guests who were starting to stare from across the lobby, eyeing me suspiciously assuming I was the cause of such antics.

After gracing this desk with an inside-out shirt earlier this week, I could not cause another scene.

"Ridiculous suggestion. Let's go."

He marched off with his family in tow, and I let out a sigh of relief that in the Midwest we rarely encountered guests with his level of attitude. I felt a twinge of pride. I had defused the situation without needing to call backup.

At 6 PM, I clocked out and went home to change for my date. We were going to go on a bike ride before ending the night at the concert in the park. They had been hosting them weekly all summer, but this was the first time we would be able to go together.

By the time we got to the park, I was ready to lie down in the grass and relax; erase the pressure of having two jobs, forget my tardy debacle, and not focus on anyone else's wants and needs for a few minutes. George had brought his biggest towel for us, a blue and white striped bath sheet he had picked up at a Target on the mainland, as well as some small snacks and a bottle of wine. We seldom drank wine, I wasn't sure if I even really liked it, but it definitely made this feel extra special for our date night.

Despite a group of our friends/coworkers/roommates sitting a few hundred yards away, George insisted this was a date, and that we should sit on our own for at least the first hour. Dusk was setting in over the lake, and the air was crisp with a chill. George quickly offered me his sweatshirt, the most subtle Mackinac Island one he could find in one of the gift stores after arriving here ill-prepared for the brisk nights. I layered my legs over his, sprawling across the towel, taking in the band which included two singers, two guitars, a drummer, a saxophone, and a keyboard player. I recognized a few of them from Bridge Bar, but they sounded even better in the open air.

Blankets covered the grass of the park, with a mix of Mackinac Island souvenir picnic blankets that tourists had picked up that day and random towels locals were willing to bring outside. It was a vibrant and colorful spread, bigger than I thought it would be, but somehow still intimate with the harbor twinkling in the background across the street.

"This is nice, but should we head home?" George suggested after about an hour of listening to the music and sipping our red wine, which I was pretty confident I didn't like at this point.

"Would love to," I smiled back, beginning to gather up our things into my pink tote bag.

We walked hand-in-hand, the large towel dragging from over George's shoulder, crossing the short distance back to the Purple House. After putting on the PJs I had been leaving in Emma's room, I started to get nervous. Was he going to expect something from me? We had never stayed alone overnight together, and—I knew without asking—George was more experienced than me.

"So I have a pretty early wake-up call tomorrow. Another double shift opening the hotel and closing the fudge shop," I shifted my weight from foot to foot and started to set the stage for why I needed to go right to sleep.

"I don't know how you are keeping up with your schedule. It is so impressive." George pulled me into a hug, wrapping his fleece blanket around me as we both dropped down into the bed. *I'm not keeping up with it.* I bit my tongue from correcting him. "I know you want a proper night's sleep, but can we at least cuddle for a little while? It's not every day Jack finds someone who isn't instantly bored to tears by him."

"Of course," I snuggled into him, using my body language to assert that cuddling was all that was happening.

George, to his credit, did not push my boundaries even a little, holding me close without ever giving the implication that this wasn't enough. Relief coursed through me as I let the tension out of my shoulders and made myself comfortable. I knew we were going to have to have the omnipresent talk at some point. I would have to tell him directly that I was a virgin, even if he already knew. I would have to tell him how far I wanted to go, even if I still wasn't sure. We would have to decide what the future had in store for us, even if there was only a month left in the summer.

But for now, we had said all we needed.

TWENTY-ONE

Mackinac Island Travel Tip #21:
Beware: The lake water is nearly freezing at night.

"ELLA! Thank goodness you are here. This shift has been absolutely prattling on, and I majorly need your advice," Emma spoke a mile a minute before I was even behind the counter. "Chase finally asked me on a date."

"Emma! That's amazing. What could you possibly need my advice on?"

Emma had two long-term boyfriends before, including one she left not too long before the summer started. There was no chance I knew anything about dating that she didn't already have first-hand experience with.

"Well, I don't always have that much to say to him. What should I do? We have very little in common at the end of the day, but I want it to be fun. Will you come?"

"Come with you? On your date with Chase?" I widened my eyes in disbelief.

"Yes."

"And you don't think that would be awkward?"

"No silly, not just you. You and George," she rolled her eyes at me.

"Oh. Well, in that case, sure. As long as Chase doesn't mind."

A double date! I had a boyfriend(ish, person) to bring on a double date!

"He won't," Emma was now grinning wider than the Cheshire Cat, clearly proud to have gotten her way. "Are you free Wednesday night? Run it by Georgie, and see if he wants to go to the Seahorse Bar & Grill."

"It's a date."

———

"ELLA, I didn't have 'go on a date with my favorite roommate' on my bingo card this summer, but this is a good surprise," Chase raised his eyebrows, discernibly unaware that his date with Emma had turned into a double. "Wait, did I text you instead of Emma? Ella, Emma could have been an easy mistake..." his voice trailed as he glanced down at his phone.

"No, you texted Emma. She didn't tell you George and I are joining?"

We were the first to arrive at the restaurant, and the host had led him to me, sitting alone at a table for four. Yikes, I guess this wasn't a double date for all parties involved. Should I leave?

"Nope, but that's okay. I'm just glad she said yes. Besides, I love my man George. Or should I say, mate?" He gave me a toothy grin, pleased with the drawl of his faux accent.

"We can totally leave if it's not okay."

"Seriously, it'll be fun."

And it was. We spent the whole night laughing, sharing stories from our craziest customers and guests, and making a bucket list of things we wanted to do on the island before the summer ended.

"Why didn't we do this earlier in the summer?" George squeezed my hand under the table in silent agreement that this should have been a weekly ritual.

"Okay, wild idea. What if we go swimming in the lake?" Chase also did not want the night to end.

The water would be ice cold at this hour, at most hours really, but I was blissfully unfazed by the concerns that usually burdened my mind.

Nodding in agreement, we paid our bill and walked through town, past the harbor, and down to a rocky beach near the glow golf course. Each of us stripping down to our underwear, we made a pact to all run in, no hesitations allowed. Lined up holding hands—Chase, Emma, me, and George—we ran on the count of three.

My high school had a charity event every year, the Polar Plunge, where people would donate money sponsoring students to jump in the Huron River at 8 AM in January. Michigan was usually about 10 degrees that time of year, and the cold chill of the water instantly shocked your body.

Even though it was currently peak summer, this water had a similarly paralyzing effect.

"You guys do know there are indoor pools and hot tubs all around the island?" Squealing in pain as the water froze me from my toes to my neck, I jumped on George's back hoping being lifted into the air would help.

"You comfortable up there, Queen Ella?" George laughed, prancing around the lake, holding me as high as he could over-head, maneuvering my legs around his neck like we were getting ready for a game of chicken.

"Comfy. Is. A. Stretch," I squirmed around, trying to keep hold of his slippery shoulders and all too aware that our bare bodies were touching in places they never had for the very first time. My attempts to steady myself had the opposite effect on George when his foot slipped on a rock, and we both tumbled, submerged underwater, a winding labyrinth of bare limbs.

"Why is it so cold?" Emma squealed. "I thought summer in the US was supposed to be warm?"

"I can warm you up," Chase ran over to her, putting his arms around her shoulders and dunking her under the water with him.

"Are you guys okay?" Emma's giggles carried across the still lake as she turned her attention from Chase to us, taking in the view of us lying captive to the frigid fresh water. My body was stiffening in the lake as if moving would use up too much energy to fend off the cold.

"Yes—"

"No," we called out in unison.

"I might never feel my toes again. Who's idea was this anyway?" My teeth chattered as I pulled my upper half out of the water expecting the night air to be warmer against my skin. It wasn't.

"That would be me. I don't know what you guys are freaking out about though, it's really not that bad," Chase was now calmly floating on his back. "Just look at the stars and forget about your toes."

George pulled me back to him, leaning us back into the water to float while cuddling. From up above, we probably looked like two little otters, floating on our backs with arms around each other, "This sky really is sparkling."

"Mhmm," my teeth still chattering. "So romantic."

"Why don't I take you home before your lips turn entirely blue?" he whispered in my ear.

"Yes, please. Otherwise, I might actually need to forget about my toes because they will be history," I mumbled the last part under my breath.

We left Chase and Emma splashing happily in the lake,

somehow both immune to frostbite, and quickly put our clothes back on our numb bodies.

"I have a crazy idea. What if I suggested we sneak into the Isle Manor hot tub to thaw?" I whined as we walked back toward the Purple House.

"I would say that the student has become the teacher," a mischievous grin spread across George's face, "and that I'm in."

We ran straight to the hotel, abandoning our now soggy clothes on the striped chaise chairs at the side of the pool. All graces gone from my body, I splashed into the hot tub without a moment of hesitation. The warm bubbling water thawed my extremities from the outside in.

"This is so much better," I wrapped my legs around George, pulling him close.

Somewhere along the way these last few weeks I found new comfort on the island—it only took a little while because I was clearly a fish that preferred the pool to the lake.

"So much better," he agreed. "Tonight was perfect."

"I know. Chase and Emma are hilarious together."

"You think they are still splashing out in the lake?" He pulled me closer, dragging his fingertips along my upper thigh.

"Highly likely."

My body was still tingling, but the cold was no longer the driving force. I craved to be closer, pulling him to me, erasing all distance between us, his woodsy cologne mixing with chlorine in the air.

"Gotta love them." He pushed my hair from my eyes, spinning me slowly in unison with the jets of the whirlpool. Kissing my hands, cheeks, and finally my lips.

Every part of my body was warm, intertwined with George, and protected from the air in an assortment of softly whistling bubbles. There was a spark between us, and I knew things would be different now. There would never be another oscillation in mood or a divide. In the last week, we had become one. We trusted each other.

We stayed for far longer than intended, unconcerned for our tomorrow selves. Each bubbling moment worth it.

When we finally tore away from each other, heading in separate directions home, my cheeks were now numb from the grin plastered across my face. I took the steps up to the apartment slowly, basking in the joy of the evening and recounting each touch in my mind.

Just as I was ready to flop in my bed, my happy bubble burst. "What the heck?" The bed was piled high with all of my soggy laundry. *Shoot, had I left it in the washer earlier?*

"You shouldn't leave your crap in the washer," Tory called from her bed before flipping to face the wall.

"Sorry." *Was she serious right now?* The passive-aggressive signs had been one thing, but the clothes had soaked through my bedding. She could have at least put them in my laundry basket. *Where was my laundry basket?* I searched the room, feeling Tory's eyes back on me as she watched with glee. She was enjoying this.

I finally found my basket, sitting right atop the washer where I left it—a more convenient spot for her to have dumped my wet clothes than my bed.

"I'm sorry I forgot my clothes, but this was extremely uncalled for," I whispered into the darkness as I threw everything in the plastic bin, knowing I would have to rewash and dry them tomorrow.

"Do you want to say that a little louder?" Tory sat up in bed, a fighting tone lacing her voice.

"You know what?" I turned to her, trying to mimic her tone. "Yeah, I do. This was not necessary. Am I sorry I forgot about my stuff? Sure, but you could have thrown it in the basket more easily than bringing it here."

"How do you think I got it all over here?" She scoffed. "I used the basket."

"You've got to be kidding. My only set of sheets is soaked through," I crossed my arms over my chest, the darkness of the room instilling a false confidence in me.

"Maybe you'll learn your lesson then," Tory laid back down, facing the wall, done with the conversation. "Sleep tight."

I could hear her satisfaction in having gotten the last word. I wanted to say more, but knew it wouldn't change a thing. Sliding into my damp sheets, I wondered what the new sign hanging above the laundry machines would say. It would probably read *promptly remove clothes, or get ready to tumble.*

TWENTY-TWO

Mackinac Island Travel Tip #22:
Bring the essentials with you because toiletries are very
expensive on the island.

"HEY, Ella. Are they making you work the night away at the fudge shop?" Jared wiped the sweat off his forehead with the back of his hand as he tossed a stack of four suitcases in the corner. I nodded, still impressed that he could take so many bags in one trip.

"Nope, I opened here today so I have the whole afternoon to myself," I grinned, as my mind wandered to all the things on my to-do list: nap, bike, see George.

"Nice! Tory and I are going to venture to the mainland and run some errands. You want to come?"

I hadn't left the island since I arrived, and despite how much I loved it here, I was starting to feel a little trapped. Plus, some of my toiletries were running low, and buying shampoo on the island would cost me approximately an entire hour of work, but I had also been avoiding Tory since the laundry incident. Maybe this could ease the tension in our bedroom.

"I'm in. Where are we going?"

"My car is parked in St. Ignace so I thought we could just stay in the U.P. Go to the dollar store and grocery store; all the hottest spots in town."

"Perfect!"

"Meet me behind the big apartment at 3:30, okay?"

Tory and I both changed out of our work clothes, putting on our least summery outfits as if it were only summer on the island, eager to rejoin the 21st century on the mainland.

"Is it weird I'm excited to be in a car?" Tory asked, putting her wallet in a belt bag and lacing up her white sneakers.

I let out a sigh of relief that we were good—she had made her point and moved on as if nothing had happened. I could do the same.

"If it is, we are both freaks," I grabbed my purse, keen to get moving.

As we headed out back, I expected to see Jared on the shore, waiting to walk to the ferry docks with us. Instead, he was bobbing up and down in a small boat tethered to the break dock.

"I knew there was a reason I was friends with you," Tory ran down the jetty, jumping into the front bow of the boat.

"Told you I'd take you on my boat this summer," Jared took my hand and guided me down into the seat next to him.

A moment later, the small speedboat jolted forward as the engine revved to life, and we were riding the waves, cruising along in the wake of a ferry all the way to St. Ignace.

You had two choices for towns to travel to and from Mackinac Island: Mackinaw City in the Lower Peninsula and St. Ignace in the Upper Peninsula. St. Ignace was the smaller of the two but offered better parking options. It was also the town that is connected to the island in the winter (they create an ice bridge lined with Christmas trees that is strong enough to hold snowmobiles) making it a natural parking choice for year-rounders, like Jared.

"There's no Walmart or Target up here, but it's not worth going across the bridge for just a half day," Jared said.

We all filed off the little boat, tying it up to a small, unmarked dock that undoubtedly was used only by those with cars in this secluded parking lot. It was very much an 'if you know you know' situation. I looked around at the assortment of cars, surprised at their presence. It's funny how much you can get so used to a new reality that your old reality can become a shock to the senses.

Piling into Jared's old Ford Escape, he put on the radio before peeling off into town. It was the first time I felt the pull of a car in nearly two months. I rolled down the window, letting the breeze of the highway kiss my cheeks and tousle my hair like an old friend.

"Shall we, ladies?" Jared pulled us into a prime parking spot directly in front of the dollar store, waving up at the sign as if this was the most shining of destinations.

"We shall." Tory opened the door and hopped out of the passenger seat.

Roaming the aisles, I filled my basket with things I needed and things I definitely did not need.

When I was a kid, my parents would take us to a 99-cent store each time we visited our grandparents in Florida. We weren't allowed to get souvenirs for the rest of our trip, but that day we could pick out five items each. I remember often selecting home decor: flip-flop candles or beach-themed picture frames to take home to my already overly cluttered room. Every year, it was the highlight of the trip for me.

This dollar store also had some decor, and I couldn't resist a picture frame with the Mackinac Bridge sculpted on it. I grabbed one for myself and one for Emma, mentally making a note to fill it with a photo of the two of us before giving it to her. Despite my basket being full of items, the total at checkout came to $14. Only two hours of work for everything I needed and then some.

Following the dollar store, we picked up some snacks at the grocery store and then drove around town for a while. Jared took us to a hidden waterfall that he said was one of his favorites to come to in high school.

"What was it like going to school on Mackinac?" I asked, genuinely curious given there were only about 500 who lived on the island year-round.

"Well, the school had fewer than twenty kids and there was only one other my age. We sat in a classroom with everyone who was in high school, and the teacher gave individual assignments based on your grade." He was evidently bothered by the experience. "That's why I wanted to go to Michigan State and get the big school feeling, but once I was there I realized I missed small-town life. Mackinac in the summer is perfect for me—I know everyone who's a local and everyone working on the island for the summer, but there are thousands of us, instead of a few hundred."

We wrapped up our day on the mainland with Taco Bell before boating back to the island just before the late evening sunset. Being on the little boat, and seeing the pastel main street of the island come into view, I realized I'd missed it. There had been moments this summer when departing the island seemed like a solution to my problems. My achy limbs, my unrested eyes, and my unrequited love. Turns out, all I needed was a few hours away to reset my outlook.

George was lying on the picnic table, watching the clouds roll by, when we pulled up to anchor the boat. My excitement bubbled up into my chest as I moved to the bow of the little speedboat.

"Hey! Are you waiting for me?" I called across the water as I grabbed the sun-faded blue boat bumpers and flipped them over the edge of the boat, pulling us up to the dock's edge.

He sat up, "Yeah, Emma said you'd probably be back soon. Are you hungry?"

"We may have had some Taco Bell on the mainland, but let's be honest that's never that filling," I admitted.

"I have an idea of something fun we can do tonight. You in?"

Obviously, I was. I thanked Jared, and we said our good-byes before heading up to my room. George was being weirdly secretive about his plans for our evening, but I changed into a flowy skirt and a chunky sweater with my white sneakers, ready for wherever the night would take us.

"Have you been on one of the horse carriages yet?" He pulled me into the crook of his arm as we walked around the building to Main Street.

"Only once when my family went to dinner at The Woods. Have you?"

"No, but I reserved a taxi for us to go to Stonebridge for drinks and dessert."

"You did not," I looked up at him with a similar look in my eyes to the six-year-olds when they entered the fudge shop for the first time.

It was really happening this time. He was quite literally waiting for me to return from the sea and ride off into the sunset on a carriage ride together. Hell, he was even British— my personal prince charming.

"Oh, but I did," he smiled, beckoning a small two-seater carriage over to us and helping me up into the main cart.

It was a yellow carriage with red vinyl seats, and there were two brown horses leading the way.

"Hey guys!" I waved to Chase and Mike as the carriage took us all the way down Main Street before turning up The Grand Hill and back into the woods.

It was a windy night, and I was glad I had worn a sweater. The horses moved forward slowly and steadily, hooves clopping on the dirt roads in a uniform pattern. We held hands, kissing in the back of the carriage for the entire 30-minute ride up to Stonebridge. The ride was bumpy along the dirt roads, but we had spent plenty of time kissing and our lips continuously found their way back to each other whenever a particularly large pothole would jostle us apart.

Rounding the bend, the mansion came into view, perfectly positioned on the cliffside overlooking the lake, the Mackinac Bridge glistening in the distance. The last time I had taken in this view was on my first outing with George, after our round of duckpin bowling, but the entire tone of this evening was different. Somehow both lighter and heavier at the same time.

"Wow. I've biked by this a million times, but never at night." I took in the view, allowing George to help me out of the carriage. We said our thank yous and goodbyes to the driver, making plans to be picked up in two hours.

"Me neither, but Tory told me I had to take you here before the summer ended."

Tory had worked here last summer and was always talking about the amazing food. Apparently, even if you worked here, you ate food prepared in the same kitchen as the restaurant, and it was one of the best perks of the job. You just had to live this far from town to claim it.

We checked in with the host and were seated in a cozy booth looking out over the water.

"This is amazing, George. What should we get?"

"How hungry are you, for real?" He pulled my hand into his lap, softly running fingers along my palm.

"There's always room for dessert?" I suggested, a lopsided grin filling my face.

"I love it. Let's get a bottle of red wine and a double

chocolate cake. I'm also going to get a steak that you can share with me." He continued to hold my hand under the table, ordering with our waitress and putting on his best charm so that we, or more so I, didn't get carded. Workers on the island usually looked out for each other, an unspoken rule that we wouldn't card in restaurant settings, but a little extra charm from George helped.

"This is the best cake I've ever had," I said, as I shoveled fluffy bites into my mouth, the sweet sensation tickling my taste buds as I savored each bite.

It was light and airy with a chocolatey cream frosting and cherry ganache on top. The red wine, which I hadn't liked at the park, complemented the chocolate perfectly, and I found myself draining my glass faster than intended.

"The best." He poured some more wine into my glass. "Cheers to the most amazing summer, with the best girl and the best cake."

"You're so cheesy."

"You know, I'm actually not. I think you just bring it out of me."

"I am highly punny, so that's certainly possible." I sipped at my second glass of red wine, surprising myself with how much I enjoyed the flavor.

He stared out the window, scrunching his eyebrows together. "Shoot," he mumbled under his breath.

"What is it?" I followed his path of sight to see what was so disturbing out there.

"It's pouring. I think the carriages don't run in the rain because the horses get uncomfortable."

"Um, are we stuck up here?" My mind swarmed with the implications of being stuck this far out of town.

"I'll call. Be right back." He stepped away, taking his phone to call our friend from the taxi stand, returning a few minutes later to confirm that we were indeed stuck up here.

"So we have two options: hike back in the rain or, and this is my preference, get a room here. I checked on my way back, and they have one available."

"Will that be, like, crazy expensive?" Staying in his room together had been one thing, but staying in a fancy hotel together was different. The implications were clear and potentially inevitable.

"Don't worry about that. If you want to stay, I've got it covered."

"Okay, let's stay then?"

He paid for our meal and then checked us into our room. When we got there, it turned out to be the honeymoon suite —because of course it was—with a bottle of champagne and chocolate-covered cherries waiting for us. It was easily the nicest hotel room I had ever been in. It was also the first hotel room I had ever been in with a date.

Growing up, my family had enough money to be more than comfortable, but they were frugal with it. When traveling, we would stay, the five of us, in one room with two double beds. My parents snored, so instead of sleeping in a bed with my sister and my mom, I often opted to sleep in the bathtub, claiming it as my private room. I would fill the tub with spare pillows and blankets from the closet and sleep like a rock.

Those nights when I opted to sleep in the tub are surprisingly some of my favorite memories from growing up, and they have conditioned me to immediately check out a bathtub as soon as I enter a hotel room. The size of a tub is an easy way to judge a room, and this one was huge. It had room for two, maybe even three, people and jets all around the edges. There was also a natural loofah and a small jar of eucalyptus bubble bath on the edge, inviting you to draw a bath.

"Well, I think we need to use this," I giggled, slipping my

clothes, undies and all, into a pile on the cold, tile floor and starting to fill the tub with hot water.

Not shy to add the entire container of bubble bath, it was foaming over the edges as we both hopped in. George poured us each a glass of champagne, and I took a tiny sip. It immediately went to my head, my heart pattering in my chest, but not in the nervous way it had other times we'd been alone together. This time it was with unveiled enthusiasm for this next step. This newfound intimacy of being completely bare-skinned for the first time, in seclusion.

"This doesn't suck," George settled in, sipping his champagne and turning on the jets.

"Not even a little. You want to know something funny?" I splashed a little foam in his direction, attempting to prolong the lighthearted mood. "I used to sleep in hotel bathtubs as a kid. By choice, of course."

"You did?" He raised his brows as if to say both 'I admire that you found that fun' and 'Wow, I hope you never have to do that again.' Even if I had a more than comfortable upbringing, he had come from old British money. And money-money like that probably did not elect to sleep in bathtubs.

"It was fun. Plus, it meant I didn't have to share the hotel room with the rest of my family. The four of them slept in the double beds, and I bunked in the tub," I smiled, not at all embarrassed by my fond memories of pillow forts in tubs around the country.

"What if someone had to go to the bathroom in the middle of the night?" he asked.

"They woke me up first," I replied, pausing to take another sip from my bubbling glass. "Usually."

"Usually?" He asked, amused. "You're not sleeping in the tub tonight."

He stepped out of the tub, wrapped me in a plush over-sized town, and carried me over to the bed, towel tightly wound. Slightly wine-drunk, I contently drifted off, George's arms a weighted blanket that halted all other thoughts. I think it was the most comfortable I had ever been.

How could I possibly have wanted off the island this morning?

TWENTY-THREE

**Mackinac Island Travel Tip #23:
Don't disturb the ghosts.**

"HEY ELLA, IS EMMA WORKING?" Chase walked into Rosanna's, surveying the shop. He had recently confessed to me that he had never been in love, girls often designating him their funniest friend before things could become intimate. I knew that this time with Emma, leaving the friend zone to be something more, was important to him.

"She is actually covering for Veronica down the street this afternoon. Want me to pass along a message?"

"Nah, I don't have much going on today, so I'll go tell her myself later. Are you and Georgie boy free tonight?"

"Yeah, what did you have in mind?" I passed him some fudge samples, reading his mind as his eyes wandered across the display.

"I actually planned out a double date for us, and I have to say, I may have outdone myself."

"Can't wait!"

Chase was creative, and I had zero clue what he would

have in store for us. If I were forced to guess, I would probably have figured it would be some kind of board game-drinking game hybrid that he invented himself...

"Toodle-loo, I'm off to tell Emma!" He waved goodbye before letting the squeaky door slam behind him.

At 9 PM sharp, there was a playfully patterned knock on my bedroom door. Chase informed me that George and Emma had just arrived.

"Hello, hello. Everyone ready for the best double date of all time?" He was adorably excited for us to all be spending the evening together.

Our last double date had been unexpected, but he was overly prepared for this one.

"I've been on a date to Amsterdam, so that might be hard to top, but we'll see," Emma loved to keep him on his toes. "So, what are we doing?"

"That's for me to know, and you to find out in about five minutes. Patience please." Chase grabbed her hand, guiding us all out onto Main Street where dusk was settling in over the island, cascading shadows across the town.

"Alright. Are you ready to know what we are doing tonight?" he asked.

"Cut the theatrics. Just tell us," Emma laughed, enjoying how much *he* was enjoying this.

"So I spent the day at the library..."

"They have one of those here?" she interrupted.

George squeezed my hand, signaling that he was as amused as I was with our front-row seat to their banter.

"Yes, and I spent my whole day off planning this date there. So you better love it."

"You spent the whole day in the library?" Emma raised her eyebrows.

"Yes, as I was saying, I spent the day in the library mapping out this date. Did you know Mackinac Island has a history of ghosts?"

"Yeah, there is a shop that does tours and things around the island. Are we going there?" George asked.

"Even better. I researched it all and am taking you on a private ghost tour. Which, if you ask me, is way spookier than walking around with a bunch of fudgies," Chase beamed with an eagerness to begin his tour.

"Has anyone ever told you that you are truly one-of-a-kind?" Emma looped her arm through his, game for the evening ahead.

"Andre tells me that every day," he chuckled at the thought of his brother. "Okay, so our journey begins here, in the center of Main Street."

Chase began his tour, detailing ghosts who lived in the theater and had haunted the main area. From there, we walked up to the Fort as Chase shined his phone flashlight and told stories about several island ghosts, including a family of kids and their father who had been stationed in the fort. I'd never been to the fort at night, but peering through the white stone wall at Main Street and the lake down below, I could see why a ghost wanted to set up shop here.

We then swung by the Post Hospital, an old white wooden structure near the fort. It is said to be the oldest hospital in Michigan and has been documented by tourists for having an overwhelmingly 'sad presence' when you enter. Sad with a side of shivering chills.

"Are you scared yet?" Chase looked to us for approval to keep going.

"Honestly?" I paused, thinking through the tone of what I said next. "Yes. I never come up here anyway, but I'll be avoiding this area the rest of the summer."

"Well just wait, the scariest is yet to come."

He took Emma's hand in his, pulling her closer to him and

guiding our group toward a large white house. We knew a few people who worked for other businesses on the island that lived there, but people tended to stick with their own company's cohorts so we had never been inside.

"And, of course, you know Mission House, but did you know this was a boarding school in the early 1800s?" He paused for dramatic effect. "There are over 15 recorded deaths among the students. We're lucky we didn't work somewhere else, or we would be living among their ghosts."

"Stop. Do you think the people who live here know that?" I gasped.

"If they ever went to the library, like me, it's pretty well advertised..."

"Do you think they ever feel the presence of the spirits in there? Or bump into a ghost when they go to the bathroom in the middle of the night?" At this point, Emma was just teasing him and going along with things.

He had put in so much effort to scare her tonight, that it was nice to see her playing the part.

"Why don't we get a little closer and see for ourselves..."

We walked around the side of the building and peered in the windows, taking in the view of the old-school architecture. Winding all the way around to the back entrance, we walked up a couple of steps, each creaking loudly. Something about the creaky steps and the way the porch fed out into the woods was spooking me. I pulled Emma's hand into mine, sandwiching myself between her and George.

"Okay, this is probably as far as we should go," Emma inched closer to Chase.

"You scared?" Chase asked.

"A little, but I also don't want anyone to get mad at us." At that moment, a guy came storming out the door to the house, dressed for a night shift at one of the horse stables. "Plus, Ella looks like she is going to pee herself."

"I do not..." I whispered to not wake the spirits.

Chase, never shy, called the guy over to us.

"What's up? You guys don't live here, right?" The guy asked.

"No, we live on Main," Chase answered.

"Cool, was worried I just didn't recognize you. There are a lot of us in here."

"Any ghosts?" Chase questioned.

"Ghosts?" The guy asked back.

"Yeah, I read a story about some ghosts living here, and we are on a sort of makeshift ghost tour, so curious if you've ever felt a presence."

"Actually, yes. Sometimes when you're sleeping here, in the middle of the night, a cool breeze passes through and it's almost as if someone is hovering over you in bed..." His voice trailed off as he took in our horrified expressions. "I'm joking! I really don't think there are any ghosts here, but feel free to go take a look around," he held the door for us and then took off.

"Shall we?"

We inched our way into the house, walking slowly, careful not to bump into anyone else who lived there. Tiptoeing around, we made our way through the hallways and up to the second floor. Legend apparently had it that the ghosts only went on the first two floors because the third was a later addition.

A cool breeze shot through the room. Emma grabbed Chase's hand, and I squeezed George's tighter as we made our way down the hallway, the hair lifting on my arms and neck. *It's not a ghost—a window is probably open,* I rationalized in my head.

The far window, where the breeze presumably entered, was shut tight. The curtains swayed gently next to it, and my grip tightened on George, cutting off any chance of circulation reaching his fingers.

"Where could that breeze be coming from?" Emma whispered as if her full voice might wake something, or someone, up.

"I have no idea. There's definitely no AC here..." Chase peered around the room, knowing full well that most employee housing didn't have air conditioning given the already chilly nights. We walked in the other direction, inspecting each nook and cranny as if there would be a visible ghost crouching in the corner. "I don't see anything."

"Me neither," my voice tremored, and George pulled me closer.

"I've got you," he whispered in my ear.

"Maybe we should head back to the big apartment for the night. I think we've seen enough of my research," Chase said.

Just as we turned to leave, all the doors in the hallway slammed shut and the door to the outside swung open. There was no scientific explanation for this; it was the opposite of Bernoulli's principle. Instead of a door slamming when a window opened, the doors all slammed and knocked another door open.

"I don't think we're wanted here," George said.

We made a run for it. Tearing our way down Main Street and to the big apartment before collapsing in a pile on the couch. No one spoke.

"So... that was the best double date ever. Right?" Chase broke the trepid silence. *Only if no one followed us back...*

"Okay fine, it was a lot of fun. But that doesn't mean I won't be squirmish the rest of the night," Emma admitted.

"I need a beer," George walked over to the fridge, offering us each a can.

TWENTY-FOUR

Mackinac Island Travel Tip #24:
There is no such thing as too much fudge.

ONE COULD EASILY ARGUE that every day is a fudge festival on Mackinac Island, yet somehow they managed to make a week in August even fudgier. This weekend was the Annual Mackinac Island Fudge Festival, a celebration dedicated to the heritage of the sweet treat, which included fudge-making demonstrations, Willy Wonka look-alikes, loads of games, live music, and fudgy concoctions that would impress even the oompa loompas.

It also included a full house at the hotel and fudge shop, meaning I would be working doubles for four straight days. You would think that I was mentally prepared based on my experience the past few months, but each day felt harder than the day prior. I woke up at 6:30 AM, put on a skirt or dress, walked down the street to the hotel, and then sprinted home at 2:55 PM to change into my polo and khakis for my shift starting at three. Rinse and repeat.

By day four, I was feeling completely detached from my

friends, and my feet felt like they had doubled in size. When I moved my neck to either side it made a slight cracking noise. I was 18 years old, and I was pretty sure this was not supposed to be happening to my body.

"Ariella, are you excited to have the day off tomorrow?" Marlani, perceptive as ever, must have noticed my dark circles.

"Yes! I am going to sleep in and then wake up and sleep some more," I mustered a smile.

"You don't want to go to the last day of the fudge festival?" she joked, knowing fudge was the last thing I wanted to look at.

"Think I'll pass."

"These events. They get cheesier and bigger every year." She mopped up the floors, looking both annoyed and amused by the idea of a fudge festival in a two-street town that already had over a dozen fudge shops. "The people love it though!"

"We gotta give the fudgies what they want," I agreed, putting my elbow and back into it as I cleaned the popcorn machine with a crumpled piece of newspaper.

"Ella! You're almost done?" The back door opened with a screech, and George joined us in the main shop.

He had started coming in the back door to say hi to me on days I worked doubles, knowing I needed to just go to sleep upstairs and couldn't hang out when it was this many days in a row. His visits had quickly become my favorite part of the day.

"I need to finish this and then wrap up some of the flavors we have left," my voice came out muffled, my head fully inside the popcorn machine.

"She's done," Marlani smirked, always quick to let me off the hook and take the overtime.

"You sure?"

"Yes, you know I don't mind, so you go along now." She was my personal fairy godmother, looking out for me and making sure my summer was still filled with movie-worthy moments, and not solely work.

"Give me ten." I knew I needed to at least finish the popcorn machine before taking off on Marlani.

"I'll be out back," he grabbed a fist full of saltwater taffy and disappeared the same way he arrived.

Fifteen minutes later, I dragged my worn-down body to the break dock.

"Hey. Was your day as crazy as mine?" This was pretty much the only question I asked after work anymore. My brain was at capacity and truly could not think of anything more interesting to say or talk about.

"Unlikely, but still nuts," George replied. A tired smile hung from his face as his legs dangled over the edge of the dock just a few inches above the water. "I've missed you this week."

"Same. I can't believe it's already the first week of August."

"Let's not talk about that tonight," his voice trailed off softly.

I had been pushing the fact that we only had three weeks left together into a very tightly closed box at the very bottom of a suitcase zipped tight at the bottom of my closet.

"Fair. Avoidance is the key to happiness these days," I laughed half-heartedly.

"What are you feeling up for tonight? There were a bunch of people back at the Purple House, or I can see if we can sneak you into the Bridge Bar..."

"I have a better idea. Let's see if Jared will take us on his boat." I point to the five-person motorboat bobbing next to the dock.

"It's kind of late for that, no? It doesn't even look like there are lights on it."

"Fine. Let's just bop around in it." I slide myself off the landing and into the boat. "You coming?"

"You're insane." George joined me, carrying a brown

paper bag that I hadn't seen next to him before. "Here, I brought us some nosh."

He pulled out fries and spicy chicken nuggets like the hero he was.

We both laid back on the white pleather chairs, looking up at the stars twinkling overhead. There was a heaviness in the air, both of us deep in thought as we munched on our salty sustenance, pondering the inevitable end to the summer.

"George," I whispered. "Do you think we will keep in touch when you go back to London?"

"I think so, Ella. Do you?"

"Yeah, I think so too."

Usually when you say something that's weighing on you, some of the weight lifts, but that didn't happen. The tension stayed in the air, hanging overhead as if a lie detector was buzzing, calling us both out on our bullshit.

———

THE NEXT MORNING, I naturally woke up by 8 AM. What was I supposed to do all day? George was working the opening shift today, so I figured I had about six more hours to kill before we could hang out. I could get a fancy coffee, but that would require mustering up the energy to walk down the street. I could go for a bike ride, but that would require changing and pushing through the fudge festival crowds on Main Street.

I settled on watching a show on my iPad in bed. This summer had been so hectic that I had barely watched any TV, but this was the ideal day for it. With *The Summer I Turned Pretty* playing in the background, the epic soundtrack lulled me back to sleep.

"Ella, Ella, wake up." My body was being gently poked

back to life. Slowly peeling my eyes open, I found myself face-to-face with Emma. "Have you been sleeping all day?"

"What time is it?"

"One. I'm on my break and wanted you to come to eat lunch with me on the dock. I never get to see you anymore, and the summer is almost over."

"ONE?"

"Yes. Are you coming to lunch with me or not?" I stared back at her in disbelief that I had somehow missed most of the second season of my favorite show, including my favorite part when Taylor and Stephen dance to Miley Cyrus, and slept through the rest of the morning.

"I'm coming, give me two seconds." I threw on some bike shorts and an oversized baby pink t-shirt. I probably wouldn't have worn something this casual anywhere other than the break dock or a bike ride, but it would do for now.

"So, the food downstairs looks kind of gross today. Can we go visit Georgie?"

"Considering I owe you for waking me up before sunset, sure. I had spicy nugs last night, but could go for a burger and diet coke."

We ran down the stairs and into the back door of Donnie's, sliding to the side of the counter and skipping the line. George was helping in the kitchen and it didn't take long for him to see Emma's ravenous eyes.

"I have so many chips. Do either of you ladies want anything else?"

"All of your fries, two cheeseburgers, onion rings, and some mozzarella sticks, please," Emma ordered for the two of us, not at all shy about asking for almost everything on their menu.

"Coming right up!" George retreated to the kitchen before returning with our greasy bags.

Lugging our to-go order out to the break dock, I felt grateful. Grateful for Emma being such a good friend. Grateful to George for providing us with an unnatural amount of food for two people. Grateful to the summer for being everything I needed and so much more.

"So, how are things going with George? You've practically replaced me with him, so it better be good," Emma asked before I had a chance to sit down at the picnic table.

"You know that's not true. I replaced everyone by working two jobs, but it's good. I think we may try long distance after the summer..." A pang of guilt tore through me.

I hoped it wasn't true. She and George had both become real friends to me this summer and if I had neglected her it was purely coincidental, right?

"You think or you know? Did you specifically talk about it?" Emma looked concerned, her big sister instincts kicking into overdrive.

"Think... We said we thought we would keep in touch last night. We're on the same page."

"Keeping in touch can mean pen pals, Ellie. I don't want to see you get hurt if he has different ideas of what that means..." She sensed the hesitation in my voice.

"I know, but we still have three more weeks here, and I don't want to come on too strong and ruin that." I looked down at my burger, no longer hungry.

"Let's go to the Fudge Festival closing party tonight, and I will help you suss it out."

"You actually want to go to that?" I asked.

"Yes! It's so cute how they go all out for these festivals here. There is even going to be an old-fashioned ice cream social in the park tonight. How darling is that?"

"We can get free ice cream anytime we want."

"True, but this will be in a park. Let's go to it. I'll bring Chase, and we will help you read Mr. Mysterious. Also, aren't you usually the one trying to convince everyone else to go to these cheesy events?" She was right—the work schedule had really worn on me.

On the one hand, I had earned plenty of work credits and just wanted to make the most of every moment left this summer. On the other hand, people were counting on me. I couldn't bail on my responsibilities, no matter how much my feet begged for mercy.

Being an adult sucked. I was ready to go back to being a kid, if only for a few more weeks.

———

EMMA HAD BEEN RIGHT, the ice cream social in the park was adorably quaint. People were serving sundaes from old-fashioned ice cream carts while wearing various pastel costumes that were right out of a classic movie set in the 18th century.

Set within the cotton candy display of twirling petticoats, were red carts concocting insanely indulgent fudge-infused cocktails. George ordered us a Chocolate Fudge martini which had whipped cream and little fudge shavings on top. It reminded me of the caramel mocha we served at Rosanna's, but fancier solely for the fact that it came in a martini glass infused with vodka.

"Was I right, or was I right?" Emma sipped on her spiked root beer float.

"You were right. This is cute," I smiled, taking in the view of the lake and the sounds of summer.

People laughing with their kids, a string quartet singing about ice cream, horse hooves trotting along the pavement, and bikes slamming their breaks as they stormed downhill from the Fort to the park.

"You excited to get back to London, man?" Chase asked George, presumably following a script of Emma's invention.

"Yeah, it's my last year in uni so it should be great. I am living with two of my mates in a new flat too, so it'll be good to get back and get settled. They both moved in already, and I just know they left me with the worst room."

"Sounds fun. I wish I could go back to school. You think you'll be back here next summer?" Still following that script, I noted with equal parts gratitude and embarrassment.

"No chance. I interned at a bank last summer and will be going back there full-time. This was just one last chance to do a summer in America."

There it was. The harsh reality cut directly to the core of what I had been so desperately trying to avoid thinking about. I sucked in a breath of air, biting my tongue as he summarized our very near reality in those three simple sentences.

In a few weeks' time, we would be going our separate ways, and I certainly would not have the time or money to go visit him in London for years. The crazy thing is, I knew this was the reality from the moment I met him and still let myself become hopeful that it could end any other way. I'm sure he understood as well, and that's why he tried to keep us in the friend zone for so long. I should have just read the signs and accepted them back in June when it wouldn't have stung this hard.

But that's not true, is it? It would sting even if we had stayed friends. The memories would be teeming with all the would've, should've, could'ves of an unexplored desire instead of the bittersweet adventures. The thing about summer love, or lust even, is that avoiding it leaves you sad and alone, but going for it also leaves you sad and alone, just a few months later with the knowledge of how great it had been.

At this moment, I wasn't sure which scenario I would have preferred.

TWENTY-FIVE

Mackinac Island Travel Tip #25:
If you have time, get on a boat that isn't the ferry.

EVERY YEAR IN EARLY AUGUST, Inez hosts a booze cruise for everyone who works across her businesses as a thank-you for the grueling efforts throughout the peak season. The night is infamous, and I had been hearing stories all week of wild incidents from years prior. People hooking up in the restrooms, puking off the side of the boat, and even one person who fell overboard a few years ago right as the boat was going under the Mackinac Bridge.

Walking down to the ferry dock where the boat would be picking us up, I was surprised to see how big it was, dwarfing the neighboring speedboats and sitting comfortably beside an idling ferry. Appearing to be over 80 feet long, we walked up to the double-decker white boat with a large "Queen Mighty Isle" nameplate across the back. The main floor was filled with tables and chairs as well as a buffet of assorted fried foods and a fully stocked back.

"Should we head upstairs?" Emma pointed to a ladder at the back of the boat.

"Let's do it." We finished the climb, greeted by many people we knew and a surprising number of people we hadn't met all summer. "Wow, it's pretty crazy we all work together, at least indirectly."

"Inez is a boss. She acts super chill, but practically everyone on this island works for her," Emma looked impressed.

"So true. I thought working at the hotel and fudge shop would mean I knew everyone here, but I guess not."

"I grabbed you a White Claw." Joining us, George handed me a watermelon-flavored seltzer. My favorite.

"You think anyone minds if I drink here?" I looked around, wondering if one drink on this boat would throw away the countless hours of work I had done in pursuit of impressing Inez and winning back her trust after the dead phone affair.

"Definitely not."

I took the can but didn't take a sip. I had gotten used to drinking this summer, but was still a lightweight and didn't want to risk making a fool of myself and becoming one of the precautionary tales that the regulars told the newbies next summer.

"GUYS! Have you seen the buffet downstairs? There are mozzarella sticks, onion rings, fries, pizza, burgers, and hot dogs." Chase ran up to us, a plate of assorted fried foods overflowing at the rims.

"Chase, you literally work in a fast food restaurant that serves over half of those things," Emma rolled her eyes.

"Yes..." He rolled his back, "But I didn't make these."

"To be fair, you didn't make the others either, mate," George chuckled.

"Whatever. I know a quality hot dog when I see one." He took a big bite, grinning through his mouthful.

"Brother, you save any for the rest of us?" Andre clapped him on the back, shaking his head.

"It's. Really. Good," he spoke through mumbled mouthfuls.

"Ladies and Gentlemen—my summer fling, Chase," Emma was so confident and quick to label their time together as just a summer thing.

No hesitation or question of what it would become when the summer ended, and I was almost jealous of her certainty; the peace she had with reality.

The horn of the boat sounded three times, and we pushed off from the dock; the engine growling loudly from two floors below.

"Ella, I want to show you something." George pulled me away from the group and over to a big bean bag chair by the front of the boat. No one else had made their way up here yet, and it was the perfect seat to watch as we rounded the corner away from the island and toward the sunset over the Mackinac Bridge.

"So who do you think is doing all of our jobs right now?" I joked.

"No one. The whole island is closed."

We laughed as if this was the most hysterical thing we could imagine, knowing it wasn't true, but also entertaining the idea that it just might be.

George pulled me back into his lap, bending the bean bag to curve around our conjoined bodies. "This really is the best sunset we've seen all summer, isn't it?"

"The absolute best." In reality, it looked exactly the same as the countless others, a watercolor of striations of pink, gold, purple, and midnight blue blended together until they faded into the horizon, but being on the boat made it the best.

Sipping our drinks, we sat in comfortable silence for a few minutes, knowing better than to take this scene for granted tonight.

"I hope you know how glad I am to have met you this summer." George pushed my hair, which had been going wild in the boat's breeze, behind my ear as we tuned out the chaos behind us of people dancing, drinking, and singing along to the music like it was a proper karaoke night.

"You know I feel the same," I nuzzled into the crook of his neck, solely focused on the warmth of his body and the sunset, but still feeling the positive energy in the air.

It was precisely what the entire summer had felt like; us in our warm and cuddly bubble, surrounded by some of the best people and energy imaginable, and I wasn't ready for it to end.

By the end of the booze cruise, no one was ready to call it a night, so most of us went back to the Purple House for more games.

"Ella and I are partners!" George ran over to secure us a spot at one end of the pong table. We were up against Chase and Emma, who we both knew usually got bored of the game halfway through, making her the perfect opponent.

"We call next!" Jared and Tory came to the side of the table, cheering us on.

After crushing Chase and Emma, we lost gracefully to Jared and Tory.

"Want to go somewhere a little quieter?" George curled his fingers around mine, gently nudging me toward the stairwell.

"Where's Jack?"

"He went into the enemy camp as soon as we got back from the boat," he said, referring to the girl from the rival fudge shop that he had been hanging out with on and off.

We took the stairs slowly, unwilling to let go of each other's hand. Entering his room, before I could even kick off my shoes, my back was up against a wall.

"Is this okay?" George kissed my neck and slowly tried to undo my bra under my shirt.

I answered with a kiss and fumbled to push my white sneakers off my feet. They landed with a thud under his bed just as he successfully unhooked my pink bra. It was the first time I hadn't undressed myself around him, and I was appreciative that he asked, not taking my comfort the other night for granted at this moment.

Wanting things to continue, I pushed George back onto his bed, untying his shoes.

"Thanks for always taking such good care of me," he laughed, leaning back on folded arms as I slid off his shoes. I loved his laugh.

"There's never an exception to the no shoes in bed rule. Especially on this island," I snickered as he pulled off his t-shirt and shorts.

Watching, I followed suit and slipped my skirt off. I was now standing in the dark in just my pink lace underwear that I had worn for this exact situation, both nervous and excited.

"Come here," George patted the bed next to him, wanting me to initiate any moves that advanced where this was going.

He knew he had more experience, and that I hadn't been entirely comfortable going even this far the other times we'd been alone in this room. Instead of joining next to him, I slowly perched myself over him, straddling his legs, and looking into his eyes. He met me halfway, and we rolled around kissing each other both in places we had before and discovering new ones.

Pulling me close to his chest, George held me tightly, tucking my tangled brown hair behind my ear, whispering, "Let's just cuddle."

"You sure that's okay?"

"Of course. I just want to be with you."

Without me having to say anything, he knew and

respected my limits. I was overwhelmed by my emotions in a good way, wanting to repay his kindness, but also wanting to cherish this pressure-free moment. He was truly the perfect guy; he hadn't even pressured me when we were in the dreamiest of hotel rooms stocked with chocolate cherries and champagne.

It dawned on me that there wouldn't always be a moment like this where I felt fully in command of what happened next. Every ounce of this decision was mine to make with no tension swaying me one way or another. It was my choice.

I could lose my virginity, here and now, on this island to a British boy who was literally better than anything I could dream up, and who I might never see again. Or I could wait, and likely lose my virginity in a dorm room to someone who could have potential and a future, but would likely not be nearly as much of a gentleman.

Facing the adorable dimple on George's grinning face, I chose now.

TWENTY-SIX

Mackinac Island Travel Tip #26:
No trip is complete without afternoon tea at the Grand Hotel.

I WENT the whole summer only biking past the Grand Hotel and never going beyond the Sadie's Ice Cream parlor and the iconic front porch, so I made it my mission to go for afternoon tea before leaving. Emma and I finally had the same afternoon off this week and had made a reservation for 3:30 PM.

I spent the longest I had all summer getting ready, carefully applying my makeup, and trying on all viable outfits. Everything had felt wrong—too casual, too business casual, too sporty—but I landed on the daisy dress I had overworn throughout the summer. It would have to do.

"I am so excited about this! We have a little tea shop in Ann Arbor that I always go to with my mom, but I have never done a full tea," I gushed as we biked up the steep hill to the Grand Hotel.

"Same. Here," Emma called as she tried to catch her

breath; she had somehow avoided biking much this summer and wasn't used to the hill.

"It is going to be amazing."

We parked our bikes in the bike rack, locking them together despite knowing there was a very slim chance anyone would take them there.

Walking through the familiar green and red ice cream parlor, we told the staff, who were dressed in old-fashioned butler-style uniforms, that we had a reservation for tea. We walked up a small flight of stairs to the main level and took in the luxurious, couture decor. There was a black carpet with red and green flowers, an assortment of eclectic green and red chairs that somehow looked like they both belonged in your grandparent's house and were extremely glamorous at the same time, and bright green walls.

We were seated at a small table with two antique chairs right in the front window, overlooking the sprawling front porch and the lake. The afternoon tea was a traditional menu, likely unchanged from the 1840s vision of an ideal tea, with petite finger sandwiches, fresh-baked scones, an array of pastries, and your choice from one of many tea flavors. There was also a pianist playing in the corner, who made the already elegant occasion feel truly lavish—like a scene from *Bridgerton*.

"Wow, this is unreal." I took in the charming seating arrangements, mixes of Victorian couches, chairs, and tables in different colors all positioned into intimate talking circles around the room. I made a quick promise to myself to one day have a colorful parlor room in my own house. Somewhere I could invite friends for a quick tea and cookies or curl up with a good book.

"I know. Very posh. I am so glad we are finally doing this!" Emma squealed. "Which tea are you going to order?"

"I think this one," I pointed halfway down the menu. "It has hints of rose, which sounds so fun and fancy."

"Love it. I am going to do the oolong." Emma fluffed out her napkin before gingerly placing it across her lap, and I followed suit.

The table was set with the daintiest little silverware that looked like it could have been made for a doll.

We ordered our teas and were swiftly served in two white teapots that were delivered along with striped tea cups with gold detailing that matched the green of the room. The serveware reminded me of my parent's fancy china, which sat idly in a cabinet 364 days a year. On the one day when it was unleashed, my siblings and I all tiptoed around the house, scared any sudden movements would destroy their most prized 25-year-old wedding gifts.

"Cheers to an amazing summer!" We lifted our cups, pinkies out, and pretended this was exactly where we belonged. Sipping tea at the most lux hotel on the island, and not mopping the floors of a fudge shop.

"I am so glad we met this summer. You have to come to visit me in Wales as soon as you have the chance."

"Duh. That would be amazing."

I was determined to save up all year and figure out a way to make it happen. I could visit Wales and England on the same trip, that is, if George would want me. The thought of what came next for us, what he truly desired, had been weighing on me even more since the night of the boat cruise. I pushed the thought aside and breathed in the rose and lavender scents enveloping the table like our own private garden, immediately understanding why people found this tea thing so calming.

"We will also need to meet up in New York City at some point."

"Bet," she quickly agreed, straightening out and then giving me a playful nudge from across the table. "What was your favorite thing about this summer, besides hanging out with me?"

"Free ice cream."

We both laughed and spent the next two hours reliving our favorite memories, all the while nibbling on little sandwiches and macarons from the three-tiered tray that had been placed in front of us shortly after our tea had arrived. I had somehow managed to do it all, even with two jobs, and I was so proud that I had stayed true to my promise to go beyond my comfort zone. It had paid off.

"But actually, it was the night in the lake. How long did you and Chase end up staying out there?" I chuckled at the memory of the four of us flailing in the icy blue water under the moonlight.

"Way too long," she involuntarily shivered, "Chase refused to leave. Even when my lips turned blue!"

"Yeah, well, he knew how to fix that," I teased, sticking my tongue out for effect.

"He certainly tried," she wiggled her eyebrows at the memory before taking another delicate sip of tea. "You know he can do this thing where—"

I cut her off, "TMI. I'm good leaving that one to the imagination."

"Your loss, love."

Emma's phone chimed and there was a sudden shift in her mood.

"What is it?" I asked.

"Ummmm," Emma looked down and smoothed out her skirt before tapping the table slowly. "I just got a DM from an old friend of mine who goes to school in London."

"And?" I tilted my head to the side, waiting for the punchline. Why did it seem like this had something to do with me?

"Well, she was asking if I knew George…"

"Why?"

"She knows him."

"And?" My palms started to sweat, and I took in two quick breaths.

"She saw him in one of my tagged photos you posted from the fudge festival, and I guess she wanted to know who you were..."

"Why was she worried about who I am?" That simple question cracked the facade of the perfect summer that I had built in my head.

"Well, he is dating one of her friends from school."

The facade smashed open entirely. Of course, he had a girl-friend. Of course, that was why he had tried so hard to keep me at arm's length and friend-zone me earlier this summer. Of course, that was why he was so patient with me. Of course, I was the biggest idiot for thinking a guy like him was actually into me. And of course, I couldn't leave this summer with only good memories. I felt sick to my stomach—stupid for ever being so naive to let my guard down.

"Look, maybe it's a misunderstanding," Emma tried to comfort me, "George is clearly obsessed with you, it's palpable every time I am with you both, but maybe it's for the best?"

"For the best?" My whole body was trembling at this point, doing everything it could to stay calm.

"Not for the best, just maybe a clean break wouldn't be so bad? You've had the magic moments, but you're going to uni soon." She put her hand on my shoulder, steadying me. "There will be even better adventures, and guys, there."

Better guys than George? Luckily for both of us, the wait-ress had placed the check on our table in the middle of this whole debacle, and we could leave.

"Emma, I appreciate what you're trying to say, but I don't think there's an upside. I just need a minute. I need air."

"I can come with you. We can get some air together, and I'll get to the bottom of this." She grabbed my now sweaty hand from across the table, simultaneously messaging her friend back with her other hand.

"Thank you, but it's okay. This tea was great, and you truly are the best thing that happened to me this summer. I just need a minute to myself," I mustered a tight smile while trying to hide that my chest was caving in around my heart.

After an all too brisk goodbye, I took off on my bike. First going up through the bluffs, cursing their idyllic image, and then taking a back road down and out onto the main circle around the island. Luckily it was approaching dinner time, and I didn't need to share the road with many others.

I glided across the pavement, hands tensely gripping the handlebars in front of me. One, two, one, two. Counting each pedal movement in a failed attempt to calm the devastation brewing in my chest, I made my way to the east side of the island.

TWENTY-SEVEN

Mackinac Island Travel Tip #27:
Make sure you bring a thick towel or cushion for the
rocky beaches.

AFTER 30 MINUTES of biking as fast as I could to clear my head, I slowed, taking in the stillness of the lake around me. I loved this lake. I was going to miss this lake. The water was serene, extending out to meet the sky as far as I could see. Ditching my bike at the side of the road, I tiptoed my way across the rocky beach, searching for a flat rock to use as a makeshift bench. The moment my butt touched the stone, the tears started. At first, I was just crying over losing George, then they turned into tears over losing a friend who I thought was so good, and finally, they turned into tears over my own behavior. How had I lost sight of the plot for this summer and made a guy my priority?

Until this moment, the most serious relationships and heartaches in my life had been with Taylor Swift's exes. I'd felt her losses deeper than any of my own and you could be sure that I was more emotionally damaged listening to a mash-up of *Dear John* and *Could've, Would've, Should've* than I was thinking about any of the guys I'd gone out with in high school.

But at that moment, I was devastated. Throughout the last four years, I always felt the losses of what I wished the relationships could have been more than the loss of the person themself. That's the thing about young love. We don't feel each loss the same way, and if someone was never right, they can leave your life without making much of an impression.

But this felt different. I'm not sure if it was his accent, his shaggy hair, or the way he just looked so effortless all the time in his maroon Donnie's t-shirt and basic khaki shorts—an undoubtedly horrendous outfit—but this was going to be impossible to move past. George was more than a summer fling; he had become one of my best friends.

Looking around, there were dozens of stacks of rocks three high; people indicating they had been here, and you weren't alone. I casually kicked one over. Then another and another. Until I had done a full sweep of my little stretch of beach.

I had never been an angry person. Seriously, when someone stole my parking spot in the school lot I usually apologized for being in their way before moving on to find another spot, but letting my frustrations out was oddly cathartic. Plus, kicking stacked rocks over hardly qualified as the destruction of property.

I collapsed back onto the rocky beach, a particularly sharp rock stabbing into my shoulder blade, and screamed at the top of my lungs as I stared up into the clear blue sky. There wasn't a cloud in sight.

My screams turned to unhinged laughter and, for a moment, I even let my mind wander to the unanswered text messages from Eric. I had felt I couldn't answer those, couldn't even let him know which days I would be home between summer and college, yet all this time I could have. George would have.

I couldn't help but feel stupid and responsible. We never made deliberate plans early on; we just met up where we knew each other would be. That should have been my first sign that something was off.

I clearly can't trust my instincts! This—this feeling—was exactly why I never pursued relationships before. I focused on my school work and my friends, and it kept me out of trouble. I should've stuck with that approach for this summer and focused on the job and friends. That had been the plan after all, and if I had just stuck with it I would still be eating beautiful little finger sandwiches right now, and I would probably still be eligible for the end-of-season bonus.

I grabbed my AirPods and turned on my favorite TS playlist, ready to wallow in the company of my idol's heartache.

With a symphony of betrayal filling my ears, I looked back out on the stillness of the water. No longer surrounded by mindful markings of other people's presence on this island, I accepted that I really wasn't alone. I had made meaningful friendships this summer (way more than George had) and I was poised to make even more in college in a few weeks. Everyone didn't know he had a girl at home, so who cares if George had played me? He had played everyone, including his other so-called friends.

I looked down at my white sneakers, they were scuffed again because no matter how hard I tried to make it so, nothing could remain untarnished. I had never let a guy's assessment of my worth influence my own attitude before, and I wasn't going to start now.

Picking up my bike with a new determination, I headed back into town. They say sometimes you just need to choose chaos, and that's what I did that night. Arriving back at the big apartment, Jared and Tory were already a few deep on the sofa.

"You're back!" Emma was also there, but she had a more sober, worried look than the others.

"Hey. Sorry for taking off. I just needed a minute," I turned to Jared. "So what are we doing tonight? Can we go to Bridge Bar?"

"Ella, you read my mind. Tory and I were going to go over there in a bit," Jared was always easygoing, so it was unclear if Emma had clued him into the events that transpired this afternoon.

Either way, I didn't care.

"Perfect." I walked over to the fridge, grabbed an open bottle of bottom-shelf vodka, and poured it into a cup with one packet of Crystal Light strawberry lemonade powder, and nothing else. Screw it! I ingested the lethal combination which tasted like equal parts gasoline and Jolly Ranchers, but I didn't care. "I'll be ready in ten."

Heading into my bedroom with my absolutely vile 'mixed drink,' I quickly changed into the sexiest outfit I had. Considering I often dressed like a colorful kindergartener, my *sexy* outfit consisted of jean cutoff shorts and a plain black crop top.

"You sure you want to go out with them? You don't want to try to talk to George first?" Emma joined me in my room, giving my outfit a concerned once over.

"Nope, like I said, I just needed a minute. I'm fine."

"Yeah, you look fine," she mumbled under her breath as we made our way for the exit.

"Jared, do you like my outfit?" Taking in his look of approval, I turned back to Emma. "See. I look better than fine."

"Ella, I've been waiting for you to have a girl's gone wild night ever since I first heard I was living with an eighteen-year-old, but are you sure tonight's the night? Did something happen?" Tory questioned. *As if she cared.*

"Nothing happened guys, can't a girl just want to have a little fun before leaving her favorite island for a whole year of classes and studying and being in freezing cold Upstate New York?"

Emma whispered something to Tory before slipping into the night. I guessed that she didn't want to stay and bear witness to my mess in the making.

"BYYYYYE!" I called after as she retreated through the after-dinner crowd on Main Street. "Let's go to Bridge Bar!"

I led the way across the street, Jared and Tory closely behind me, both giggling at my newfound attitude. They had both likely led a small parade of people to a bar on a moment's notice many times in their lives, but it was quite obvious this was my first time.

Following them through the crowd of people, we squeezed our way to the front of the bar.

"Two light beers and," Jared turned toward me, "what's your favorite drink?"

"Ummm, Shirley Temple?" I replied.

Jared laughed, "And a dirty Shirley."

Drinks soon in hand, I followed Jared and Tory back through the crowds.

"Ella, you ever play darts?" Jared asked, balancing his full, frothy beer pint in one hand and picking up red darts in the other. "I'll show you how."

I was more interested in my dirty Shirley than the game, swirling the floating cherry around on the top of my bright red drink. This was good. Why hadn't I tried this before?

"No, but I have never tried one of these before and it is ah-maz-ing. Like so good."

"I'm glad you liked it," Jared laughed, running his fingers through his hair and shaking his head at me. "Come here."

For some reason, he believed it was a good idea to teach me to throw sharp objects at a time like this.

"I'll play for Ella in the first round," Tory grabbed the blue darts from my hand.

My head moved back and forth, a metronome ticking away, as Jared and Tory took quick turns throwing.

"I win," Tory grinned tightly. "Ella, the trick is to keep your elbow close to your body and just be the dart. Picture it flying to the middle, and it will."

"Okay, sure..." I got up, ditching my now empty glass on the table next to us, trying to make sense of that horrible explanation. My first throw landed on the floor before even reaching the wall with the dart board. "Whoops!"

"I'll get more drinks," Tory slinked off toward the bar as Jared corrected my form, giving me the oh-so-helpful advice to throw farther on the next go.

By the time Tory made it back with our refills, I had gotten exactly one dart to stick to the outer ring of the board.

"Wahoo! Look at me go. I am good at this," I hollered, unaware of the crowd that had started to line up behind us.

"You're good at everything, Ella!" Tory chided, and through my hazy state, I couldn't decipher the sincerity of the statement. "James, from the yacht race, is here. I'm out."

"Guess it's just us," I turned my attention back to the dartboard, eager to figure out the trick and make the bullseye.

Regardless of her tone, Tory was right. I could be good at everything. I just needed to practice.

"Ella, you ready to go home? Where'd Tory go?" Emma cut through the crowd, grabbing my arm to steady me.

"The yacht man came back. He liked her. He might have a girlfriend at home too, but she doesn't care," I spun around in a circle, before falling into Jared's lap in a pile of giggles.

"Emma, can you help me out here? She is way too drunk

right now." Jared really was a good guy, even if he was a huge flirt.

Emma, the true friend that she was, lifted me with Jared's help and started dragging me out of the bar.

"Ella, are you okay?"

We had barely made it to the curb when George arrived. *What the actual—? How dare he intrude on my night. And when I was just starting to get good at darts, too!*

"I am FABULOUS. Not that you care," I let a small burp through a trail of giggles.

"Clearly. Can we talk?" George asked.

"You really think now is the best time?" Emma questioned on my behalf.

"Well, no. But I also can't wait for tomorrow. At least let me help you," George said.

Three people were now dragging me by my limbs down what might be the literal most charming street in America, and I was dead weight.

"Can you tell I have had a lot of fudge this summer?" I giggled again, this time snorting at my own joke. "If you haven't had the dark chocolate sea salt caramel, you need to try it. I will probably fill my suitcase before I go home."

"You think you're being funny, but I am actually going to do that," Emma smiled, seeing this sloppy side of me for the first time.

"Don't worry, Emma. I'm going to visit you and we'll be friends forever. I can bring you more fudge when you run out. I'll just have to come back here first..." I prattled on, finding plot holes in my own plans.

It was a bit of a bumpy ride, but a few minutes later I was back in my apartment, flopped across on my bed. Jared left quickly, likely heading back to the bar to salvage his own night, but Emma and George stuck around. First changing me into my pajamas and then helping me brush my teeth.

"Emma, do you mind giving us a few minutes?" George willfully requested.

"Anything you want to say to me you can say in front of Emma!" I flung my arm over her shoulder, both of us now sitting on the edge of my bed, a united front.

My legs were now hanging over the edge, swinging in the air like a little kid.

"Okay. Ellie, you know how much you mean to me. I am so—" George softly pulled my hands into his.

I pulled my hands back aggressively, "I don't know anything about that. I hear there's someone else who means just as much, probably more."

"There's not. Emma told me what happened when you guys were at The Grand. Please, at least let me explain." I looked up, wide-eyed and ready to fight at the next lie to come out of his mouth. "I had a girlfriend during the school year, but she dumped me in April. She spent the summer in Barcelona and didn't want to be with me. I took the break up kind of hard, which is why I didn't make a move on you at the beginning of the summer, but I promise you, I never cheated on you. Or cheated on someone else with you."

There was a sincerity to his voice. His eyes were wet, his expression pleading, and I desperately wanted to believe him.

"What do you think, Emma? Do we believe him?" I kept my own tone sharp, disguising my inner thoughts.

"I actually do. While you were at Bridge Bar, I called my friend and got more details. His ex had reached out, trying to get back together after seeing the photo of the two of you, but he said no."

"Hmmmmm," I turned my head back and forth between the two of them. "You should probably leave, George. The room is spinning, and I am not sure if I still care if I puke on you or not."

"I'll stay," Emma climbed into my twin bed, snuggling under my pink floral quilt.

"You really think I should forgive him?" I whispered once I was sure the front door had clicked closed behind him.

"I think you're an amazing person, and I also think he is a great person, so yeah, I think you should forgive him. That doesn't mean I think you should stay with him, but I think you can take the next week to decide. End things on your terms, and then go off and meet some other smarty pants at Cornell. He can still be a good person and a good memory, without being your person."

Emma really was wise beyond my years.

TWENTY-EIGHT

Mackinac Island Travel Tip #28:
Bring Dramamine if you get seasick.

THE FOLLOWING MORNING, I wasn't ready to take Emma's advice and forgive George, but I had a double today and needed to try my best to let it go. Not necessarily fully, but at least enough to smile my way through the next 16 hours.

Clocking in at 7 AM at the hotel, I made a silent wish that things would be chill that day and that I wouldn't have to sneak away mid-shift to puke. Naturally, that meant I had cursed myself with a terrible shift.

"I need help," a man with curly brown hair ran up to the front desk, and my head was already throbbing. *How did people regularly drink this much?* "I feel seasick. Someone needs to come to my room immediately. The floor is wobbling."

"Hi sir, I am so sorry to hear you are having a tough day. Can I please ask you to explain the exact problem so I can best assist?" I myself felt quite seasick, but refrained from asking my real question which was: *are you also drunk or hungover, sir?*

"I already did. The floor isn't flat in my room. It is making me completely seasick. I need someone to come to see if they can put a beam in it and level it out."

"The floor isn't level?" I couldn't hide my confusion.

"Don't be so dense. We are on an island, and the floor isn't level. It's giving me such seasickness. You must hear this all the time."

No, I really did not hear this all the time. "Would it be helpful if I sent a porter up to see what's happening with the floor?"

"Only if they can bring some wood and tools to level it out immediately, or I'll have to leave. This whole island really is wobbling. I thought it would float more steadily," he narrowed his eyes, and I felt certain that if this was a cartoon there would be steam coming out of his ears.

Did he really think the island was floating? "So sorry sir, I am not sure I am understanding. You think the whole island is floating?"

"Clearly, that's why everything is off balance." I bite my tongue from explaining that the island was actually fully connected to the ground; like all islands, it was a mass of land in the lake and not a floating rock. "So are you going to send someone, or what?"

"Someone will be right up."

A mischievous grin spread across my face as I spotted Jared unloading his haul of suitcases on Main Street. He would be the perfect person for the job.

"Hey, Jared!" I waved him over. "We have a guest in need of assistance in room 303. He says the way the island is floating makes the floor in his room off balance. He needs you to level it out right away so that he stops being seasick."

"You're joking," Jared slapped the top of the front desk, eyes wide, waiting for the punchline.

"Not even a little." We both erupted into laughter and last night's festivities inched their way up my throat before I swallowed and choked back my amusement.

"Well, I guess I better hurry then before he floats away," he smiled, always thrilled to deal with the weirdos. "How are you feeling by the way?"

"I'm okay. Thanks for taking care of me last night," I looked down, wondering exactly what I had said and done in front of him and just how embarrassed I should be.

"Don't mention it. You are a very fun drunk."

"Oh gosh. What did I do?"

"There was just a lot of singing. You're not very good at it, by the way. But seriously, don't worry about it. You were great entertainment, and no one got hurt," he chuckled. "I'm going to head up there."

"Please come back here immediately and let me know how it goes."

About 45 minutes later, Jared was back and said that the man would be checking out soon and leaving the island. It wasn't the way he remembered from his last visit and nothing could cure his seasickness.

"I hope nothing was actually wrong with him that he's mistaken as this." I gave him the benefit of the doubt.

"No, his daughter was mortified and said he complains everywhere he goes. He just doesn't like it here and is hoping you'll comp his room."

"Not a chance. We are fully booked, and someone who actually wants to be here could have booked it if it weren't for him."

Before I could deal with conveying that message to our oh-so-seasick guest, my phone chimed.

MARA

Would it be crazy if I came to hang out this weekend?

ELLA

Not even a little.

This was perfect timing.

Windermere Point hosts movie nights throughout the summer on a large blow-up screen, and I had been dying to go all summer. The thing not everyone realizes about Michigan is that it is at the most western end of the Eastern Time Zone. This means that the sun sets incredibly late, especially in the summer. In late July—that means after 9 PM. So going to movie night is actually a late night, but not late enough to be easy to work around the closing shift.

I checked Instagram to see what classic movie would be playing this weekend and was thrilled to see *Mamma Mia!* would be gracing the big screen. Thank goodness it wasn't anything too obscure. Mara and I had actually learned the choreography of *Super Trouper* when we were sophomores, so it was perfect for our reunion.

ELLA

Four words.

Mamma Mia Movie Night.

MARA

Getting in the car now ;P

"Ella, can we talk?" George, looking as if he had slept even less than I had with deep circles ladening his eyes, quickly approached the front desk. My heart sank, his presence evoking a warmth over me despite still not being ready to have this conversation.

"Now is not a great time, George. I have a very upset

guest who is on his way down here for my help." I had officially found someone I wanted to talk to less than Mr.
Seasick.

"Okay, but I'm not leaving until I know that you have the
right details. My ex and I split before I even stepped foot on
this island and met you. I would never have played you—or
anyone. You know that, right?"

"You know, I don't know if I know that, but I am
choosing to believe it. I just really don't want to talk about it
right now. I'm working."

"I swear to you, it's the truth. Can we please talk more
when you're done here?" he pleaded.

"I'm working a double shift today, and will probably be
too exhausted," I sighed, mumbling this last part, "And frankly
I just won't feel like it."

"I'll meet you at midnight. On the break dock," he walked
away, not leaving me a chance to respond.

Who did he think he was? This was ridiculous. Taylor
Swift was the only one worthy of being met at midnight.

During my evening break at the fudge shop that afternoon, I made a sad turkey sandwich to eat at the picnic table.
Our cook clearly made sure his day off was today so that my
dinner could match my mood.

"Oh honey, that's not a dinner," Marlani shook her head
as she joined me at the picnic table.

"It's fine." I looked out at the water, choking down each
bland bite slowly.

"What's got you so down? You're usually the most positive one around here," she asked, her voice laced with genuine
concern.

"Well, George isn't as dreamy as he looks," I lamented.
"He's your average boy after all."

"That accent is dreamy," she laughed in agreement.
"What'd he do, though?"

"It seems like he has a girlfriend back home. Or maybe he doesn't, but either way, he didn't tell me about her."

"He either does or he doesn't. There is no gray area there," she paused, waiting to see if I would respond before continuing. "You can't concern yourself with things that happened before he knew you. If we all did that, no one would ever find a match."

"Do you think we all have one perfect person?" I asked, curiosity spiking my voice.

"No. I think we can choose anyone to love and cherish as a partner. My husband is a great man. I love him dearly, but it's not always easy. I come here every summer, and he takes care of our son. In the winter, I am at home, and he's mostly working. Most of the time, he is my life partner more than he is my husband, in the romantic sense. That doesn't mean I don't love him, but if I only loved him, and we didn't have the rest going for us, it wouldn't be enough. A true partnership needs a deep trust and reliability in addition to the love."

"Yeah, that makes sense," I sighed again, picturing a future where I never found that—bouncing from one unreliable person to the next.

"Look, you don't need to pick someone you can rely on right now. You're young, you're lucky. Pick someone who makes your life more fun, and then when you meet the right person, who makes life fun and you know you can count on, marry them."

"Thanks, Marlani."

"Anytime, dear. I know it seems like a big deal now, but years from now, he will just be the British boy you lusted after for a summer. Don't feel like you need to make it anything more or less right now. Enjoy it."

As we were wrapping up our shift for the night, Inez came into the shop. Ever since my screw-up at the hotel, I had been slowly trying to win her back.

"Hi, Inez. How's your evening going?" I plastered on my biggest smile and my best posture.

"It's lovely out." Inez passed an envelope addressed to Cornell University over the fudge counter. "That should put a dent in your work credit hours. You've earned it."

"Thank you," I looked into her eyes with what I hoped conveyed deep gratitude. "Especially for giving me a second chance to prove I could handle it."

"You know, I was worried we were putting too much on your plate when we first brought you to the hotel. I didn't want you to miss out on the fun the island has to offer, so a small part of me was glad to see you were still enjoying life. Screwing up is part of being a kid, and one mishap isn't an indicator of who you are and what you can achieve."

Relief coursed through my veins as she walked away. Despite it all, I had achieved my goal in coming here and salvaged my relationship with Inez. As I did a final lap around the store before closing, I found a second envelope. Ariella Abrams was scrawled across the front in Inez's loopy cursive. My forehead wrinkled as I tore into the paper, pulling out a check.

$1,000.

The memo line stated: *Something extra for the extra 220 hours that you took on with a smile.*

It had all been worth it.

———

AT FIVE TO MIDNIGHT, I peeked out the blinds of my bedroom at the dock. There he was, sitting calmly at the end of the plank waiting for me. I was so far over this day and the splitting headache that had come with it that I considered not going. I could just leave him out there and keep peeking to see how long he waited. It would serve him right, wouldn't it?

That wasn't my style though, so I slid on my flip-flops and marched down the stairs, ready as I'd ever be to hear what he had to say.

"Hey, you came," George looked up at the sound of my sandals flip-flopping against the slotted wooden dock.

"I considered bailing, but you looked so sad out here that I figured I could give you five minutes."

"Thank you." We sat in silence, both looking down at our reflections in the dark water below. Usually, we both had too much to say, but that wasn't the case this evening.

"Why didn't you ever mention her? If it was really over?" I broke the silence with the main question that had been weighing on me all day, and a pang of regret tore through me. I shouldn't have been the one to speak first.

"I thought about it a few times. Especially at the beginning of the summer, when we were just friends. I could tell you were interested in more, and I wasn't ready. So I took it slow and resisted the urge to vent to you about my ex. Did you really want to spend your summer with some guy whining about all the ways he'd been hurt before? Plus we were having so much fun together. Talking to you was the highlight of my day, and I didn't want to change our dynamic." I finally looked up from the water, allowing myself to look into his deep hazel eyes. They were more pained than I had ever seen them. "Then, we went to the glow golf course, and things changed between us. It didn't seem like there was any reason to tell you I had a relationship before meeting you."

We sat for a minute, letting everything he said sink in. *Pick someone who makes your life more fun.* Marlani's words stuck with me. George had made this summer the most memorable of my life. He would make my last little bit of time here more fun, and I didn't need to expect anything more from him beyond that. "That's all fair."

"You get it?" George straightened up, his hazel eyes fighting off the storm clouds with sunny hope.

"I do, but what happened this week when she reached out to you?" I couldn't just let him off the hook—no matter how cute his accent or singular dimple was.

"She messaged me, having seen a photo of us, and asked if we could get together when I got home."

"Oh." They had a history and would be back at the same school in a matter of weeks. Would his feelings for her return when they inevitably bumped into each other?

"I told her I wasn't interested. I know we may not leave this summer together, but either way, I know I don't want to get back together with her."

"Yeah?" My heart was torn. I was relieved that he knew their chapter was closed, but there was still so much uncertainty for us. I wanted to lean into the fun and listen to Marlani's advice, but that had never been my strong suit. I was a planner through and through. Could I let myself jump and fall without a clear safety net?

"Obviously, Ella. Can you really not tell how special you are to me? How I have clearly never felt the way I do about you with anyone else before?" His fingers were now looped through mine as he turned his body toward me, our knees touching.

"Honestly, yes. I really can't tell. You have this whole other life, and I don't. It makes it easy to doubt things."

"I guess I will have to do a better job showing you just how much you mean to me the rest of the summer. Can you please let me?"

"I think I can handle that," I leaned closer to him, a slow smile reclaiming its rightful home on my face. "Why did you pick midnight anyway? I could've met you at eleven."

"I was hoping the new day would give me a better chance

at your forgiveness," he beamed, a twinkle of the moonlight catching in his eyes. "Seems like I was right."

We sat there, shoulder to shoulder, knee to knee, legs dangling above the water taking in the peace of the moment for a while longer. I felt lighter than I had all day, certain that we could end this summer on a high. Meeting George and falling in love—or whatever this was—for the first time had never been my plan. It was an unexpected outcome, a subplot to the larger story, but it had also been magic. I wanted to remember us like this moment: steady and content.

TWENTY-NINE

Mackinac Island Travel Tip #29:
Leave time to shop on Main Street. The boutiques have a
little of everything.

"HEY ELLA, Emma, Marlani. How are you ladies doing this lovely morning?" I was mindlessly folding fudge boxes the next morning when George came into the shop.

"Someone is happy to be back in your good graces," Emma whispered, elbowing my side.

"Can we do something fun this weekend? Just us?" George looked wistful, like a toddler who had just finished his time out and wanted to play again.

"About that... Mara is going to come this weekend, so I won't have much free time."

"Don't worry. I will just third-wheel you guys," he smirked, leaving with a handful of saltwater taffies.

That evening by the time I got off work, Mara was waiting for me upstairs. She had always been good at making herself comfortable, so I wasn't surprised to find her flopped on the couch watching reruns of our favorite show.

"YOU'RE HERE!" She jumped up, pulling me into the biggest hug.

"No, YOU'RE HERE!" I squealed back.

"Yeah, the door was unlocked so I made myself comfortable. Chase was just here too. He is really funny, do you know that?"

"He is the best."

"Okay, well tell me everything. I got your panic texts and your nevermind texts, but I have not forgiven and forgotten so catch me up. Who do we hate?"

I told her all the details. The feeling of betrayal, the inevitability of life outside the island, and the current state of my mostly given forgiveness.

"So we don't hate anyone, but we are treading lightly back into things with George," I summarized.

"I support it, but not for the reasons you might think. George has been the PERFECT summer fling. Truly, a London boy who works next door and lives with half your friends? Sign me up. It's perfect; however," she paused for dramatic effect, "I don't think you should stay together post-summer. I know you are practically in love with him, but you are going off to college. Let it be a good summer memory and if you somehow find your way back together later, it's kismet."

Why did people keep saying this to me? I looked down at my lap, unable to meet her eyes, and clutched my body to hold myself together. She was right and we both knew it. She'd said all the same things Emma and Marlani had, but I hadn't been ready to accept them until I heard them from her. Since the day I met her, Mara had always known what was best for me.

"You're right," I sighed. "But have you heard his accent?"

We both erupted in giggles, Mara put on our shared playlist, and we danced around the room getting ready for our night. The tone of the evening changed so easily, with the simple act of her presence getting me out of my own head.

"This is so cute!" Mara squealed as we approached Windemere Point. "I can't believe you got to do this all summer."

"I actually got to serve fudge and handle guest complaints all summer. This is my first time here," I looped my arm through hers.

"Well, I'm glad I could be here for it then."

Arms still linked, we wove our way through the crowd of tourists in the grassy field looking for the perfect place to set up our blanket. Selecting a spot off to the right, we had a solid view of the screen with the lake sparkling in the background.

"Emma is going to come to meet us too," I smiled, happy to have my favorite people together for a girl's night.

Emma had never seen *Mamma Mia!* before, and I couldn't wait for her to take in the musical magic of ABBA.

"Hello, lovelies!" Emma swung her pink tote bag down next to us and laid down on the blanket. "I brought some rosé. It seemed like what you American girls would love for a movie night."

"You're the best."

We poured our pink wine into red solo cups and toasted an amazing end to the summer as the opening scene filled the screen. We sat back and allowed ourselves to be transported to Greece.

"I can't believe how good that movie was! How had I never seen it before?" Emma gushed as we walked back through town and to the Purple House.

It was nearly midnight, but with Mara in town and tomorrow off from work, our night was only just beginning.

"I hope everyone understands if I take over the music when we get there and play exclusively ABBA for the rest of the night," Emma wiggled her butt, dancing down the sidewalk.

"We can just tell them it's Mara's birthday, and she

couldn't possibly celebrate without the full *Mamma Mia!* soundtrack playing in the background."

Walking up the white porch steps, we all swayed a little, tipsy from our rosé. I wanted to capture this moment, me and my two best girlfriends, having a time without needing anyone other than each other. I had always been a girls-girl, and times like this reminded me why. When you find true friends, you can bond over the simplest things. There are no confused feelings, no pretending to be anything you aren't, and no hidden agendas. You don't need to second guess whether you're being cool or chill; you don't need to hide emotions. You can just be entirely yourself.

Still in our moment of bliss, we crashed through the front door and into the living room I had gotten to know so well this summer. Seltzers acquired, we cranked up the Bluetooth speakers and brought the rest of the room into our happy bubble.

"George! You remember Mara, right?" I threw my arms around his neck, not showing any signs of the tension from earlier this week.

"Of course I do." He pulled me closer while turning all of his attention to Mara. "How's your summer been, Mara?"

"Good, better now that I am reunited with Ariella. You know she's the best, right?" It was said as a compliment but also meant as a threat.

A reminder of how good he had it, and that Mara was watching his every move.

"I am well aware. She has been the absolute highlight of my time here in the States."

"Good," she gave him one last look up and down before grabbing my arm and pulling me toward an empty area to dance.

Emma joined, the three of us turning the living room into

our own personal karaoke studio. Sophie and Veronica were quick to make themselves part of our sing-along and before long everyone was belting out ABBA at the top of their lungs. At one point we all ended up standing on the worn couches putting on a show while using our white skinny cans as mock microphones.

The hours ticked by, and the seltzers flowed. George tried to pull me out to the porch or up to his room, but I had no plans to leave the living room. Mara and I would also be going our separate ways this fall, me to Ithaca and her to the University of Michigan, and this really felt like our last chance to be together. We ended the night the only way we knew how—with pizza and breadsticks.

THE NEXT DAY, I took Mara to all my favorite spots on the island and made sure she got the full experience. Emma was working, so she lent Mara the yellow bike she had been borrowing from Inez for the summer, and we made it around the whole place. We even ended with lunch at Fort Mackinac.

Fort Mackinac was founded during the American Revolution when the mainland, Mackinaw City, was deemed vulnerable by the British. From what I understood, the Americans and British switched off who was in control for a while, and then it was returned to the United States after the War of 1812 ended. It was an active base until 1895 when it closed and the island transitioned from being a center for fur trade into the summer resort destination that it is today. Now, the fort is open as a living history museum with various reenactments, exhibits, and a café run by the Grand Hotel.

Mara and I split a turkey croissant and kettle chips, overlooking the lake from the Fort above. You could see everything from up there, and it made sense that it was such a great spot for soldiers to be stationed, with a clear view of anything threatening the island.

"So what should we do tonight?" Mara asked, mid-bite.

"I think a bunch of people are coming to my apartment tonight, so we could do that? Maybe grab dinner somewhere on the water before?" I suggested, always happy to make plans for our next meal before the one we were currently eating had finished.

"Fab. Anywhere you haven't tried yet?"

There was a little bistro near the ferry docks that had been on my list, and we quickly made plans to go there that night. Once we gobbled up every last kettle chip, we hopped back on our bikes and went down to Main Street and spent the rest of the afternoon bopping in and out of all the stores. We always loved shopping together, both of us are major Maxxinistas, and this would be one of our last chances to go before the school year started.

"You need this for welcome week," Mara held up a black and white checkered mini skirt in the boutique.

"Should we get matching ones?" I grabbed one in my size to try on. "Also, it's called o-week for me."

We went to the University of Michigan's Welcome Week last year, posing as freshmen and leading actual freshmen around campus to fraternity basements.

"O-week. So fancy," she rolled her eyes at my future school's abbreviation for orientation week. "But yes, we are obviously getting matching ones."

She grabbed a skirt and before long our arms were loaded with stacks of clothing to try on. Stuffing our hauls into one fitting room, we tried on each article of clothing, examining it from all angles. Shopping with us required patience as we searched for the best items and best deals, never rushing the process.

Two hours later and ready for dinner, we checked out. Both of us had carefully selected three items to take home, including the matching checkered skirts.

THIRTY

Mackinac Island Travel Tip #30:
Plan ahead if you want to visit the Round Island
Lighthouse as it is only accessible by kayak or private
boat.

GEORGE

Meet me out back when your shift ends. I
have a surprise…

ELLA

Should I change for a bike ride first?

GEORGE

Nope, just come straight here. I have an
outfit for you.

ELLA

Kinky

GEORGE

Welp, now we will both be disappointed by
the surprise

I WONDERED what it would be. We had been almost everywhere on the island at this point, but maybe he made another fancy reservation? His stories from London did make it seem like Donnie's was not the kind of place he usually ate, and I wouldn't put it past him to have made some very elaborate dinner plans.

"Marlani, do you need anything before I leave? Emma?" I checked in with the closing crew, before taking the door out to the back, winding through the mess of deliveries that had arrived in the storage room that day.

As I swung open the wooden door, I was greeted by the most unexpected site. George, standing in the middle of the dock, wearing a blue and black wetsuit, holding a hot pink wetsuit that looked about my size.

"What are you wearing?"

"The same thing you will be in a few minutes," he ran back to shore, a lopsided smile on his face as he held the wetsuit up to me. "Go change."

"Where are we going?" I hated wetsuits and only wore them when absolutely necessary. The thick scuba material was always tighter and stickier than I wanted.

"It's a surprise," a sly grin spread across his face, bringing out the singular dimple on his left side. As always, he looked adorable.

"The wetsuit wasn't the surprise?"

"Nope, but trust me; you'll want it. The water's cold tonight."

"Whatever you say, captain," I grabbed the suit and went upstairs to my room to change.

As expected, it was a little snugger than comfortable, despite being the right size, but I squeezed it on over a hot pink bikini I had purchased when Mara was here.

"I look ridiculous," I walked down the jetty to meet George, noticing for the first time that he was fussing with a purple and orange Jet Ski tethered up to the end of the dock. "Who did you steal that from?"

"I borrowed it from a friend," he said proudly. "Well, it actually wasn't so much a friend, but a customer. A high schooler who summers on the island with his family. We traded."

"What could you possibly have had to trade with a high schooler?" I asked as if I hadn't been a high schooler two and a half months ago. "Not that I am complaining because this is amazing."

"He wants to impress a girl with a private dinner in Donnie's, and I told him I could make it happen. He has a Jet Ski, so I don't know why he thinks Donnie's is the way to impress her, but he seems to have gotten the idea on TV."

"Her loss, our gain." My entire face was glowing as I got on the back of the Jet Ski, wrapping my arms tightly around his torso.

We both had plenty of room on the yellow and orange seat, but I scooted as far forward as I could, planting myself tightly on George's seat.

"Okay, hold on." He fumbled with the key a little more and started to jolt us off away from shore. He was a little choppy like it was the first time he had ever driven one of these.

"Have you done this before?" I kept my voice calm, trying my best to hide my concern.

"Eh well, we don't do this much in London, so not exactly."

"Lean left. I'll take over," I shimmied around him on the right and positioned myself to drive. My grandparents had retired to a small lake in Southeast Michigan, and I had learned how to drive a jet ski at 13 years old. "Now, you hold on tight."

I took off, leaving a flowing wake of water behind us, the splashing sound wrapping me with a sensation of deja vu. I started zipping around, going away from the center of town and toward the harbor. It felt so good to be on the water, and George had been right about the wetsuit. It was keeping me warm.

"Wait, you don't know where we are going," George called over the howling wind.

"Aren't we just bopping around?" I felt fully in my element and thrilled to be able to show him the ropes of something for once.

"Nope, go toward Round Island."

"Are people even allowed to go there?"

"You really need to ask fewer questions. Can't you let it be a surprise?"

"Okay, okay! I'm going." I took a very quick U-turn and started us on our way to Round Island.

The island was uninhabited and featured only an adorable white and red lighthouse. The one time I left the island over the summer, it was the first thing I saw on the way back before the island crept into view.

As we inched closer to the island, I slowed down to just about five miles per hour, gliding across the top of the calm lake, "Which way?"

"To the left. There's a little beach you can pull up to."

I maneuvered over to the beach, attempting to avoid the rocky bottom. George hopped into the water, picked me up off the Jet Ski, and tied the hoist to a post that had magically appeared exactly where we needed it. Taking my hand, he guided me down the beach to a red and white checkered blanket and woven picnic basket.

"Oh. My. Gosh," my jaw dropped. "How did you do this?"

"I had a little time this afternoon to come set it up. Do you like it?" His eyes filled with apprehension. *How could I possibly not like this?*

"Like it? This is the absolute sweetest thing anyone has ever done for me," I stood up on my tiptoes to give him a quick kiss before turning back to the blanket with a squeal of excitement. "Wait, how did you get over here if you don't know how to jet ski?"

"Ariella, my family summers in Greece. I am very comfortable on a Jet Ski. I knew you would like to drive, but wouldn't want to if you thought I also wanted to. You're too nice like that."

He anticipated everything, always planning ahead, just like me.

"Wow. This is amazing," I slid off my wetsuit and put on a sweatshirt that he had conveniently packed in the picnic basket before taking a seat. "You really thought of everything."

"I wanted us to have a perfect last date. I know there's still the bonfire tomorrow, but I wanted this to be special. Just us."

He pulled out a mini cheese plate, equipped with grapes, jam, and nuts, as well as a bottle of champagne.

"I feel so posh," I laughed, testing out an accent on the word posh and taking a sip of my champagne. "You've really been slumming it eating hot pockets with me this summer."

"Not at all. I am going to severely miss broccoli cheddar hot pockets when I get home."

Home. We had been avoiding the topic since we had made up, but now it was hanging in the air again, right in front of us.

"I'm sure you can find them somewhere in London," I tried to keep it light, but the mood had shifted at the mention of his home across the pond.

"It would hardly be the same." We both avoided eye contact, unsure if the other wanted to actually discuss the obvious elephant on the island. Picking at the grapes, I tried to wait him out. "Look, Ella, I know we haven't talked about it much yet, but can we wait a little longer? This night is about who we are to each other right now, and who we have been all summer. Can we leave who we are to each other tomorrow to, well, tomorrow?"

"Deal," I smiled tightly, trying to push the elephant off the island and into the lake. "Can I have a little more bubbly?"

Somehow, we both succeeded in living in the moment: reminiscing on our favorite moments from the summer, times Jack came home completely plastered, and my adventures learning to understand Tory's insane quirks. By the time we were done with our snacks, the sun was starting to set, casting a stunning mixture of orange and pink through the sky.

"If you could do anything with your life, what would you do?" I comfortably lay with my head on his shoulder, sprawling out across the checkered blanket.

I looked up into his eyes, eager to hear his response.

"Is 'be an investment banker in London' a boring answer?"

"Yes," I laughed. "What would you actually do?"

"Hmmm," he pretended to be really thinking about it before scrunching his nose up as if he'd landed on the optimal scenario. "I'd buy an island and open ten fudge shops and twenty hotels."

"Hey, I was being serious!"

"I would seriously be an investment banker. Maybe even dabble in real estate."

"That is so boring," I laughed, secretly jealous that he knew exactly what he wanted to do and was already set to do it.

"At least I'm on the right path. What would you do?"

"This is going to sound so cheesy, but I want to be a wedding planner. I've seen a few come through the Hotel Waldenwood this summer, and it seems like the best job. You get to make all these small beautiful moments come together for a couple, and they'll remember it forever," I felt a blush creeping to my cheeks. "Sorry, that's so mushy of me."

"Not at all. I think you would be amazing at it."

We both lay there, thinking about our futures, mine hypothetical, unknown, and his set in stone to begin exactly as he wants next summer.

"You know, I actually do like your idea of buying an island and setting up a whole town," I thought out loud. "Inez is—quite literally—a boss, and I would love to own a bunch of different shops and restaurants. Maybe I'll be an entrepreneur one day."

"You're going to crush anything you try to do."

I don't think he realized how much his words of affirmation meant to me, but I filed them away in my brain, promising myself that one day I would go for it.

"We should probably head back before the sun fully sets, and it gets too dark to jet ski."

We changed back into our wetsuits, grunting as we pulled them on—which was an even bigger challenge now that they were wet—and stowed the basket and blanket in a surprisingly large compartment in the front hood of the jet ski. George took the wheel this time, and we slowly made our way back to the island, neither of us wanting this night to end.

"So how did you realize we could go over to Round Island, anyway? I haven't heard of anyone going there," I asked as I stepped back on the dock.

"I am embarrassed to admit that the kid who lent me this jet ski had the idea. Apparently, his family does it all the time."

"You are full of surprises."

An expansive feeling filled my chest as we made our way to shore.

THIRTY-ONE

**Mackinac Island Travel Tip #31:
Complete your trip with a visit to the Mackinac Island
Butterfly House.**

THE END of the summer had approached faster than anyone wanted. I felt burnt out from work, but I also wasn't ready to leave my friends. There was still more to do on the island—I hadn't even made it to the Butterfly House yet—and there was George. Sweet George. We had an amazing picnic last night, but tonight was our final night together on the island. I would be heading home tomorrow to give myself a few days to unpack and repack for college.

Most everyone else would also be leaving in the next few days, so tonight we were having a bonfire to close out the summer and say our goodbyes. Andre had planned it up near Fort Holmes, the highest point on the island, in a field that had a fire pit, and we would all be biking up there after work. I was closing, so would be one of the last ones to make it, but George had offered to wait for me to bike together.

"Marlani, thank you so much for everything this summer. I loved working with you."

We hugged in the back room of the shop, her clocking out for the evening and me clocking out forever. She'd finish the season this fall before spending the winter at home in Jamaica and returning here next summer to support her family.

"Ariella, don't tell the others, but you were my favorite," she smiled. "Can you promise me one thing?"

"Anything."

"Give school your everything this year, and don't come back next summer. You have such a bright life and so many opportunities. Don't waste them."

I had spent my day thinking about all the reasons I was sad to be leaving this island, and she had spent hers knowing she would be back year after year, having to leave her family for a five-month stretch because the opportunity and savings she could make here would provide for them the remainder of the year.

"I promise," I squeezed her hand and made her promise to keep in touch, sending me regular updates on her son, in return.

At that moment, I made a second promise to myself: to enjoy tonight and do exactly as Marlani advised. To go home tomorrow, and not feel sorry for myself. To pack my things, and appreciate how much lies ahead of me. To cherish the memories of the summer I was privileged to have and to remember each moment as a happy memory, including the ones where customers were yelling at me.

After a quick change, I ran out back to grab my bike and made my way over to the Purple House. Like so many other nights this summer, George was waiting for me on the front porch and swiftly joined me on the road.

We spent the first few minutes biking in silence, both aware that this was going to be our last night together, likely forever. I wondered if he was having as much trouble as I was focusing on the present.

"How was your last day of work?" George broke the silence.

"Good. Saying goodbye at the hotel was pretty easy, but saying goodbye to Marlani was tough." We were biking nearly straight uphill, and I was too short of breath to elaborate. "Do you know which way we're going?"

"I think it's this way."

We turned on a narrow, muddy path, continuing to bike uphill, my breath catching in a steady stream of puffs. This was an area of the island we somehow had not found before, but we knew it was the tippy top so figured upward was the right direction. We let the smell of smoke and the sounds of our friends guide us until we came to a clearing in the woods.

"Finally! You guys made it," Emma gushed, running over to greet us with two drinks in her hands. "You need to catch up."

"Cheers!" I took my watermelon hard seltzer and clinked it against my friend's cans. Looking around, I confirmed that everyone was there. Mike and Andre were looking cozy on a flannel blanket, Jared and Tory were goofing off next to the fire, Sophie and the other girls from the boutique were posing for photos together, and we were here; standing together atop our favorite island with the summer breeze passing quietly.

"Will you let me make you a proper s'more?" George grabbed a stick and a marshmallow, admiring the large fire in front of us.

"If by proper you mean burnt, then yes. It's the last night of summer, and I need a perfectly crispy marshmallow—burnt on the outside and gooey on the inside."

I snatched a stick and started on one.

"You're right. This is good," George leaned over and took

a huge bite of my s'more, still waiting for his own marsh-mallow to very slowly turn a golden brown.

The move brought a smile to my face, memories of our first kiss filling my mind.

"Hey now! Make your own." I gobbled up the rest of mine, and within minutes, was covered in sticky marshmallow guts.

"Ella! Come here," Emma called from across the lawn.

"What's up?" I ran over, leaving George by the fire.

"We need you to settle a debate for us. Would you rather… a customer with five kids who are all yelling for different things at the same time, or a customer who is alone but takes ten minutes to decide what they want?" She was in a group of five girls from the fudge shop, and they seemed to have been playing a full round of 'Would You Rather?'

"Easy. The kids. Before you have a chance to get too annoyed, they are gone."

"See! I told you all," Emma high-fived me, pleased to be on the same team.

"Okay let's all play a game," Andre came up, beckoning us all to come to sit around the fire. "Everyone tells a story from this summer, it can be anything you want, that was horrible at the moment, but now you love thinking about it."

"How about how people asked me if the Kahlúa fudge tastes like Kahlúa every damn day?" Emma called out. "I've never even had Kahlúa before, but I always told them it tastes exactly like it." Everyone laughed. "What? They always agree that it does after they sample it! We give endless free samples, why should I describe how things taste?"

"Or the people who come into the clothing boutique and ask if we have any coats on sale?" Sophie chimed in, moving a little closer to the fire. "No, we are closed from October to May every year. We don't sell coats or have leftovers from winter on sale."

"I love the people who ask if when they make their order a meal, it includes a drink. Yes, the same as every other fast-food restaurant you've ever been to," Andre added.

"Okay, my favorite is the families that ask for a room with a queen bed and a pull-out instead of two doubles... and the kids are teens who have to take the couch," Tory, always a lover of the drama, smiled slyly.

Jared's hand was resting on her thigh, and I wondered if there was more going on there.

"I had a man who felt sick because the island was 'floating' funny," I used air quotes around floating, enjoying the chorus of my friends' laughter in the woods.

It was such a corny game, but everyone's stories were great. Some people told embarrassing moments, others difficult customers or stories of times they missed the ferry back over and barely made it to work.

"Should we sneak away?" George whispered in my ear.

I wanted to keep listening but also wanted to be alone together, especially after last night.

"Yeah, let's go."

With a hasty exit, we grabbed our bikes and started on the journey back to Main Street. It was much faster than the ride up, and we approached the Purple House less than 15 minutes later. It was already 2 AM, but the others probably wouldn't be back for a few more hours.

"Come on," George grabbed my hand and instead of leading me up the stairs and to his room in the Purple House, he guided me in the other direction toward the harbor.

We walked out onto the harbor docks, a place I had been numerous times this summer, but never with him. We slid our shoes off, legs dangling over the edge, and spent the next couple of hours talking. About any and everything. It felt like we were desperately covering any topic we hadn't had a chance to explore yet this summer, and I loved every second of it.

"My family made plans for us to go spend a week at the beach in Spain when I get home," he stared out into the distance, telling me about his family and their annual summer vacations.

He filled the silence between us with tales of what he was going to do when he got home, and all about his college roommates and their plans for senior year. Picturing him on spring break in Ibiza was like imagining an entirely different world.

"Wow. I'd love to go there one day," I splashed the water with my toes, visualizing him at a fancy beach resort with a DJ playing all hours of the day.

"It's much easier to explore Europe from London. It's the same as you going to Florida. You'll make it there one day."

He held my hand in his lap, drawing circles on my palm with his fingers. Leaning against George, my mind wandered to the pros and cons list I had made earlier in the day.

Pros + Cons of Asking George to Keep (or Start?) Being My Boyfriend

Pros

1. This was the best summer ever, in large part due to him

2. He is really sweet and smart

3. I've always wanted to go to London (we could probably have a fancy tea there...)

4. His accent and dimples

Cons

1. The distance would make it impossible to see each other more than once a year

2. I'm moving to college next week

Despite the list of pros being longer, I knew the cons held more weight. At that moment, we somehow both subconsciously agreed not to broach the topic of staying in touch. Sure, we could have committed to texting or calling with updates, but instead, we said nothing. Both knowing that after tonight it was unlikely we would have a chance to see each other for years, and whatever happened would be for the best.

Sometime later that night, we went back to his room and fell asleep cuddling on his little twin bed, as we had so many times in the last couple of weeks. When I woke up the next morning, he was still snoring softly. Instead of waking him, I gave him a little kiss on the forehead before sneaking out, tiptoeing carefully down the stairs with my white sneakers dangling off my wrist before sliding them on and rushing down the street to pack my room.

All summer, we never said I love you, but it was an unspoken understanding, both of us knowing the end would be harder if we cemented those words by saying them and acknowledging what was already so obvious. Sneaking out this morning was just another way I could protect my memories and my heart. Our unspoken goodbye the night before would be so much sweeter than anything I could say now.

THIRTY-TWO

Mackinac Island Travel Tip #32:
Take lots of photos. You won't want to forget the magic
of Mackinac.

THE HUSTLE of Mackinac Island was not going to take a rest, even for my last day. Between throwing everything I own into a suitcase and making my rounds to say goodbye to everyone who was still here, other than George whom I continued to avoid, I was running out of time.

Emma was working, but I swung by to pick up some fudge to bring home for my family and friends.

"I love you," I squeezed her tight, the words coming easily.

"I can't wait to be reunited somewhere in Europe sometime soon," she promised, arms wrapped just as tightly around me.

"It's a date," I smiled, thinking back on our many double dates and friend dates this summer.

How was it possible we had only been friends for three short months? She passed me an overstuffed bag of all my favorite fudge flavors, broken out into four boxes of three that

I would easily giveaway over the next week before I made my way east.

The heavy fudge bag sat on my bed as I gathered the rest of my belongings together, squeezing it all back into the duffles I came with. By the time I wrestled the last zipper shut, sitting on my bag and breaking into a light sweat, it was time to go.

I looked around that room that had become my home, taking a mental picture of the twin beds, dressers, and most of all—the view of the lake. This room had been daunting a few short months ago, a place that was new and contained uncertainty. Now, it was filled with memories of all the ways I had changed that summer, all the new experiences I had welcomed. I pulled on my white sneakers, which were once again polished and scuff-free ahead of our journey home.

"You are an absolute lifesaver!" I gushed as Jared entered the apartment, ready to help me move out just as he had helped me move in.

We hustled down the pier, barely making it in time for the ferry I had promised my mom I would be on. As the ferry pulled away from the dock, I took in the shoreline one last time. Main Street was quiet given the hour of the day, each pastel building sitting side by side like a safe haven from a world where things did not always fit together so perfectly. The Grand Hotel was perched atop the hill, sparkling as the crown jewel of the island.

In the end, I had been right—this was a summer I would remember forever. As the island went out of view, I let the waves of the ferry crash over while I dozed off for a few minutes—dreaming of what might come next when I headed off to school.

By force of habit, I started making a mental list of all the things I wanted to remember about the summer. The feeling of biking alone early in the morning, the smell of sugar mixing with milk in a copper cauldron, the sound of the screen door slamming behind the last customer of the night, the view from the front desk out onto the main street. Each moment at the Purple House, laughing in the living room with friends I felt I had known far longer than a few months. The names of the horses I pretended to know up in the bluffs.

"ALL ASHORE."

I was jostled back to reality as our ferry boat was tied up, the gravel lot now visible, my mom waiting with open arms.

As the radio began to crinkle with static and the trees thinned outside the window, I knew we were getting farther. That was it. My first summer alone. Living on an island. My saved tips were not likely to last even the first month at school, but the memories of fudge-filled days would stick with me.

After all, there's nothing quite like spending one summer on Mackinac.

ACKNOWLEDGMENTS

First and foremost, I'd like to thank Mackinac Island for providing the unrivaled inspiration for this story. The island stirred these decade-old daydreams of mine, and I know Ariella and George would not have come to life on these pages without that influence.

And to you, dear reader: Thank you for believing in the magic of Mackinac. I am in absolute awe that anyone wanted to read this book and am forever grateful that you made it this far. I hope you enjoyed the journey to the island.

To my editors, Hannah and Sabrina: Thank you for your skillful feedback and commentary. Working with you both was an amazing learning experience and has turned this book into one I am proud to publish. Working together has been so rewarding, and I hope we get to do it all again soon.

To my parents: I could not have done this without you. Thank you to my mom for always encouraging my wild imagination. Whether we were painting on the walls of our basement, sewing stuffed animals for a holiday market, or launching a blog (before they were a thing), you have always played make-believe with me. I am grateful that you were the first to read this book. Thank you to my dad, who taught me I can achieve anything I set my mind to. Whether you were teaching me to build a dock, use proper grammar ("anyways is not a word"), or play golf, you have made it clear that with a little practice, I could do it all. Thank you both for always taking me to the school book fairs, and sorry for that time I secretly bought dozens of books on your credit card before you knew how Amazon worked.

To my husband: You have supported me wholeheartedly in this endeavor, often believing in this book more than I did. Thanks for cheering me on, listening to my endless rambles dissecting various teen love stories, and reading your first YA rom-com. There are more words, but I have already said them to you. I love you for infinity.

To my sister and brother: Thanks for always playing with me and letting me tag along. Many fond memories of our adventures together on the lakes of Michigan influenced this story. Melanie, thank you too for your help on my cover design. Your comments made it so much better.

To all my beta readers, both family and friends: You're the best. You read this book when it was still an incomplete shell and helped shape it into what it is today. Thank you for your immensely helpful reactions and for letting me babble on about this project in the past year. I love you all so much.

ABOUT THE AUTHOR

ALANA ROBIN is the debut author of ONE SUMMER ON MACKINAC.

As a graduate of Cornell University's School of Hotel Administration, Alana has always had a passion for hospitality. She has spent her professional career focusing on hospitality operations, change management consulting, and commercial real estate strategy. Her goal as a writer is to share her passion for travel and hospitality careers with young readers through novels that transport the audience to each book's dreamy destination.

Born and raised in Ann Arbor, Michigan, she spent the summer of 2013 working in a fudge shop and hotel on Mackinac Island and has daydreamed about writing this story ever since.

Alana now lives in New York City with her husband and visits Michigan as often as possible.

Connect Online
byalanarobin.com

 instagram.com/byalanarobin
tiktok.com/@byalanarobin

Made in the USA
Las Vegas, NV
14 May 2024

89941924R00146